MW00655647

“I ne[illegible]**athlessly** as she tried to keep her distance.

Noah shook his head as he reached for her. “You need something else altogether.”

She pressed back against the kitchen counter, but he captured her by the waist with one hand and pulled her to him.

“What do you think you’re—”

“Be quiet, Maggie. Just be quiet.”

“But—”

He smothered the sputtering sound she made, silencing her with his mouth. His beautiful, sensual mouth. He fed on her like a man starved for the very essence of her, and she couldn’t drink deeply enough from him.

He tore his mouth free, then drove his fingers into her thick hair as he framed her face between his palms. She stared up at him, desire glazing her wide blue eyes and flushing her skin.

“I want you. . . .”

WHAT ARE *LOVESWEPT* ROMANCES?

They are stories of true romance and touching emotion. We believe those two very important ingredients are constants in our highly sensual and very believable stories in the LOVESWEPT *line. Our goal is to give you, the reader, stories of consistently high quality that may sometimes make you laugh, sometimes make you cry, but are always fresh and creative and contain many delightful surprises within their pages.*

Most romance fans read an enormous number of books. Those they truly love, they keep. Others may be traded with friends and soon forgotten. We hope that each LOVESWEPT *romance will be a treasure—a "keeper." We will always try to publish*

LOVE STORIES YOU'LL NEVER FORGET
BY AUTHORS YOU'LL ALWAYS REMEMBER

The Editors

Loveswept® 772

SEDUCED

LAURA TAYLOR

BANTAM BOOKS
NEW YORK · TORONTO · LONDON · SYDNEY · AUCKLAND

SEDUCED

A Bantam Book / January 1996

LOVESWEPT and the wave design are registered trademarks of Bantam Books, a division of Bantam Doubleday Dell Publishing Group, Inc. Registered in U.S. Patent and Trademark Office and elsewhere.

All rights reserved.
Copyright © 1995 by Laura Taylor.
Back cover art copyright © by Barney Plotkin.
Floral border by Joyce Kitchell.
No part of this book may be reproduced or transmitted in any form or by any means, electronic or mechanical, including photocopying, recording, or by any information storage and retrieval system, without permission in writing from the publisher.
For information address: Bantam Books.

If you purchased this book without a cover you should be aware that this book is stolen property. It was reported as "unsold and destroyed" to the publisher and neither the author nor the publisher has received any payment for this "stripped book."

If you would be interested in receiving protective vinyl covers for your Loveswept books, please write to this address for information:

Loveswept
Bantam Books
P.O. Box 985
Hicksville, NY 11802

ISBN 0-553-44511-1

Published simultaneously in the United States and Canada

Bantam Books are published by Bantam Books, a division of Bantam Doubleday Dell Publishing Group, Inc. Its trademark, consisting of the words "Bantam Books" and the portrayal of a rooster, is Registered in U.S. Patent and Trademark Office and in other countries. Marca Registrada. Bantam Books, 1540 Broadway, New York, New York 10036.

PRINTED IN THE UNITED STATES OF AMERICA

OPM 0 9 8 7 6 5 4 3 2 1

Writing not only provides me with
an outlet for my creativity, it also
allows me to express my affection
for those people who enrich my life
with the gift of friendship.
One such person is David Bennett.
This book is dedicated to him as he
celebrates his fiftieth birthday.

ONE

Maggie Holden made her way to the front door of her Monterey home, her goal the early-morning edition of the Saturday newspaper. She planned to enjoy it as she indulged in a leisurely breakfast, something she rarely had the opportunity to do during the regular school year.

She smiled. Life seemed very simple on this, the first day of her summer vacation. For the next ten glorious weeks, she would be free of adolescent female students, lesson plans, and faculty meetings. She intended to spend the time puttering in her rose garden and catching up on the books she'd been stacking on the night table beside her bed for the last several months.

Maggie spotted her paper, but she also spotted something else. Or rather, someone else. Her smile instantly faded and her hands fell limply to her sides. Frozen in place in the doorway, she stared at the man who leaned against the railing that circled the veranda-style front porch of her modest home. She watched him lower her newspaper. Stunned, she blinked, certain she was hallucinating, but he didn't disappear. If anything, he seemed even more real.

Maggie almost ducked back inside. Her heart raced as shock spun recklessly through her. She couldn't believe her eyes even as her gaze took in the man's rugged features and the smile tugging at his mouth. His sensuous mouth. A mouth the legions of women he'd dated had invariably commented on when she and Noah had worked together many years ago. But that had been in another life, she reminded herself, and they had been different people then. At least, *she* had been a different person—a trusting person.

Her hands knotted in the fabric of her ankle-length silk caftan, she whispered, "Noah Sutton."

His smile broke free. She realized in that moment that he was still one of the most attractive men she'd ever known. He had to be forty now. There was just a hint of gray at his temples, but his dark hair was still dense and cut short. Tall, lean, and muscled, he looked more fit than most men ten years his junior. She suspected that he still kept in shape on the tennis courts of the international community that welcomed both his engaging personality and his legendary skill as an economist.

"Looking for this?" he asked as he folded the newspaper into a tidy rectangle.

Still speechless, Maggie nodded.

"You used to be an early riser," he remarked.

"Only when duty called." The words passed her lips automatically.

"I've surprised you."

"You've startled me. There's a difference." She warily asked, "Why didn't you telephone first?"

Noah shrugged. "I'd hoped that it wouldn't be necessary to make an appointment to see an old friend. Besides, your number's unlisted."

"It's been a long time, Noah."

How, she wondered, had he found her? She didn't bother to ask the question; powerful people were capable of accomplishing whatever they wanted, and Noah Sutton was one of the most powerful men she'd ever known. A respected economist and foreign trade negotiator, he'd made a name for himself as a national advisor.

He nodded, and his hazel eyes lost some of their luster. "Almost six years. An embassy party in Paris, if memory serves."

His reference to the event unnerved her. Of course he would remember, she realized. He couldn't be expected to forget the scene in the receiving line at the charity gala cohosted by the American and French ambassadors. Her late husband had baited Noah with coarse remarks about the elegant model he'd escorted to the party.

She'd never understood the cause of the antipathy between the two men, but she clearly recalled the humiliation she'd suffered that night, and on many other occasions. Humiliation caused by her husband's deteriorating judgment and alcoholic excesses.

Shaken by the memory, and a thousand others that were equally painful and deeply seared into her soul, Maggie worked at clearing her mind of the past. She'd learned long ago that she couldn't change what had happened, nor could she have avoided being tainted by her husband's acts of treason and subsequent murder by his coconspirators. The past—her past—was a part of classified government documents. That only a few people knew the specifics failed to soothe her in the least.

Noah approached her, first handing her the folded newspaper, then extending an empty coffee cup from a fast-food restaurant. "I could use a refill."

She briefly glanced at the cup. "This really isn't a good time for a visit."

She'd reclaimed her maiden name, moved as far from the diplomatic scene as possible, and started over. Why hadn't that been enough? Why wouldn't people leave her in peace?

"We were good friends once, Maggie. Doesn't that count for anything?"

She paled. His was a legitimate question, but she didn't know quite how to respond. Common sense urged her not to encourage him, but, in the end, curiosity and loneliness prompted her otherwise.

What harm could there be in a brief encounter? An hour of chatting about nothing in particular? Then he would leave, his curiosity appeased, and she would return to her solitary life.

She'd worked for this man as a translator during her tenure with the State Department prior to her marriage, and they'd run into each other at various embassies across the globe during the years that had followed. He'd never been the kind of person to indulge in cruelty. Praying silently that he hadn't changed, Maggie summoned a hesitant smile. "Come inside, Noah. I've just put a fresh pot on."

"I was hoping you'd say that." Following her as she led the way into her home, he asked in a charming, hope-filled voice, "Any possibility of one of your world-class breakfasts for an old friend?"

She might have teased him about his lion-size appetite, which apparently he still had, but she didn't. His reminder of the friendship they'd once enjoyed made her question her impulsive decision to invite him in. Three years ago rumors of treason had swirled around her. She'd become persona non grata, shunned by everyone, including those she'd considered friends. The risks of trusting, of depending on others, were too great, she found out. Now she maintained her distance from people.

She didn't know how much he'd learned about her fall from grace, and she wasn't altogether sure she wanted to find out. She had no intention of discussing the situation with Noah or anyone else. Not ever. Had he suddenly reappeared in her life without any warning just to reclaim a lost friendship? She seriously doubted it.

In the cozy kitchen at the rear of her home, she concentrated on preparing asparagus and cheese omelettes, but her hands shook with nervousness. She forced herself to go slowly, thinking through each step, while Noah stood nearby, drinking coffee. Uneasy under his watchful gaze, she put him to work setting the table. As the English muffins were toasting and the omelettes cooking, she decided to microwave a dozen strips of bacon. The heck with cholesterol awareness. She needed all the fortification she could get at the moment.

She felt grateful when Noah concentrated on his food after she brought their plates to the table in the alcove adjacent to the kitchen. Other than his occasional groans of pleasure, which she took as a compliment to her culinary skills, they ate in relative silence.

"You haven't lost your touch," he said once he finished eating.

She darted a look in his direction. "Thank you."

He reached for the coffeepot. "Refill?"

"Please."

7

Noah filled both their cups. "You're very quiet," he observed.

She shrugged, trying to appear relaxed. "Just hungry."

"How have you been, Maggie?"

"Fine," she said. "And you?"

He frowned. "Very good, as a matter of fact."

"Are you still with State?" she asked in an effort to get away from monosyllabic replies.

"Not any longer, although I still do some consulting work for the secretary and the president."

His reference to the secretary of state and the president of the United States reminded her once again of the power he wielded.

"I'm running my own shop now."

"You always wanted that," she commented.

"My headquarters are in Zurich, but I don't spend much time in the office."

"Are you still rescuing third world countries from the brink of economic collapse?"

He smiled. "Only when they're wise enough to take my advice."

The rigidity of her spine eased a bit at his good humor. "I see your ego is still intact."

"Last time I checked." He paused, studying her with characteristic intensity. "What about you?"

She froze, instantly guarded once again. "What about me?"

"What kind of work are you doing these days, Maggie?"

She heard simple curiosity, but her voice sounded strained even to her when she answered. "I teach."

"Let me guess. French, Italian, and Russian."

"Mostly French and Italian."

"What about German?"

"There isn't much call for it among my students."

"You're gifted. Very few people ever master so many languages."

She shook her head. "You know my parents were linguists. They were wonderful teachers when I was a child."

"You've never given yourself credit for the discipline it takes to remain multilingual," he observed.

"Perhaps, but it's hard to take credit for something that comes so naturally."

Uncomfortable that Noah felt inclined to touch on the talent that had brought her to the diplomatic community in the first place, she abruptly stood. She wouldn't ever be able to return to that community, and mourning the loss was a waste of time.

Gathering up her dishes, she walked into the kitchen. She wanted him to leave and prayed he would take the hint.

Instead he followed her, depositing his dishes on the counter beside the sink. "Can I help?" he asked as he stood beside her.

She inhaled shakily, taking in the subtle, but

masculine scent of his cologne. It summoned a response she hadn't felt in years, a response that had nothing to do with the past but had everything to do with the fact that he was a man and she a woman. Her hands trembled as she turned on the water, and she clenched them into fists in order to steady them under the flow of water.

Noah embodied sophistication, intelligence, and virility. Secure and successful, he never needed to make others feel insignificant in order to elevate himself. If anything, he'd always seemed capable of bringing out the best in people. She hadn't ever thought of him as anything more than a good friend, but now . . . now she saw him as a man capable of stirring her passions, and it shocked her.

"Would you like help, Maggie?"

Flushing, she refused to meet his gaze. "No thanks. I can manage just fine by myself."

She knew she sounded rude, but she couldn't help herself. Noah frightened her, and she hated feeling afraid. She'd been on intimate terms with fear for far too long.

"I like your home. You always managed to bring a sense of style and warmth wherever you lived. You worked a small miracle in that converted warehouse in Kenya."

"Thank you." A nester at heart, she took pride in her home. That part of her personality hadn't changed. It was probably the only element of the old Maggie Holden that had survived.

"Your roses are remarkable," he said, commenting on the rose garden visible from the window above the sink. "I remember how much you used to love the long-stemmed Mr. Lincolns. I see you still do."

Startled by his memory of her passion for roses, she glanced his way. His rugged profile showed a man who was the product of sturdy New England stock and a childhood spent on the ski slopes of Vermont. Harvard had beckoned to him as a young man, and he'd answered the call. His younger sister, whom Maggie met more than ten years ago, had observed that Noah wasn't the kind of man to be held back when he set his sights on a goal. Maggie suddenly wondered about the goal he'd set for himself in Monterey. What exactly did Noah want from her?

"How is Jenny these days?" she asked, taking herself in hand. She didn't feel inclined to make a fool of herself by revealing her loneliness or her startling attraction to a ghost from her past, a ghost that was achingly real.

"She's just had her third daughter."

"That's wonderful." Maggie's throat closed. Babies. She longed for children, but during her marriage, the timing had never been right.

She made herself smile at him before she returned her attention to the dishes. "She must be very happy. Congratulate her for me the next time you speak to her."

He nodded, his gaze bordering on the speculative as he watched her. "I will."

Without being asked, Noah helped himself to a dish towel and began to dry the dishes. Too busy grappling with her reaction to his physical nearness, Maggie didn't object.

She told herself that her response to Noah was the result of the isolation of her life, but the lie didn't sit well with her conscience. Honesty prompted her to conclude in the privacy of her thoughts that a woman had to be deeply in love with another man or made of stone not to feel desire for Noah Sutton.

"I have an excellent memory, but I'd forgotten how beautiful you are," he suddenly said.

Shocked, Maggie dropped the omelette pan. It clattered against the rim of the sink and then plopped into the soapy water. Gripping the counter edge, she turned to look at him.

Noah smiled at her. "I'm not making a pass at you."

She felt the fluttering of the pulse in the hollow of her throat. Her poise departed. "Then what exactly are you doing?"

"Stating the obvious, I suspect, so take a deep breath and relax. I'm not the first man to comment on your appearance, and I doubt I'll be the last."

"No games, Noah. I don't know how to play them, and I don't plan to learn at this late date."

He chuckled. "You make yourself sound like a relic when you say things like that."

Maggie glared at him.

He grinned at her. "You're a thirty-five-year-old knockout, so quit behaving as though you're over the hill."

"Thirty-four, and I'm not over the hill, but I have rules for my life that you're about to break."

"Tell me about your rules," he invited. He folded the now-damp dish towel and draped it over the handle of the stove. Leaning against the edge of the kitchen counter, he studied her with a calm that infuriated her.

"I'll print up a list for you," she said.

He gave her a steady look. "I'm not a threat, Maggie."

"I have my own personal definition for the word *threat*."

"That's not surprising," he remarked mildly.

Her chin rose, and her pride kicked in. He *did* know, she realized. "What do you want from me?"

"The pleasure of your company."

"I don't understand."

"Don't you?"

Maggie couldn't believe what she'd heard. "Are you asking me out on a date?"

"Yes, I'm asking you out on a date. Have dinner with me tonight. I've discovered a great restaurant near the pier."

She floundered, completely caught off guard. "Why?" she whispered.

"I'm bored with my own company," he confessed.

When she still hesitated, he added, "Take pity on me, for old times' sake, if for no other reason."

The charm that would have seemed like an act with any other man rang true with Noah. *Unbend a little*, her inner voice prodded. *You'll probably have a nice time. You haven't been out for a meal in months.* "All right."

He took a step toward her, reached out, and gently gathered her into his arms. He was solid, an utterly unexpected source of comfort. She felt warmth flood her veins, turning hot and steaming as it moved through her slender body. Maggie trembled, hunger for Noah rising up inside her like a tidal wave.

A strained expression on his face, Noah loosened his hold a few moments later and peered down at her. "I've missed you, Maggie. I've missed the sound of your laughter, and your ability to make the people around you feel valuable. I've also missed your smile."

Her chin wobbled. Tears welled in her eyes, but she blinked them back as he released her. She fought for control, determined not to fall apart. Extending his hand, he stroked her cheek with his fingertips. His expression was an odd blending of compassion and something she couldn't identify. Her eyes briefly fell closed, and she let herself savor the gentleness of his touch. He withdrew his hand, and she felt the absence deep in her soul.

"I'll pick you up around six," he told her.

She sighed and nodded, but she didn't move. Instead, she watched him turn and walk out of the kitchen.

The sound of the front door closing jarred something fragile deep within her. No one had touched her with tenderness or kindness in many years, and the humor that had once been an integral part of her personality had been buried under an avalanche of pain long ago. The latter was as rusty with disuse as her emotions. With no family to turn to, with no one standing at her side when the crisis had unfolded three years earlier, and with the understanding that she was forbidden by the State Department to discuss the case with anyone, she'd withstood the destruction of her reputation and her world. Alone.

No one had stepped forward to help her. Trapped and terrified and fearful of incarceration in spite of her innocence, she'd been too emotionally devastated to reach out for assistance. She'd remained alone—a virtual island in a tumultuous sea of uncertainty and disdain, a subsequent recluse so badly wounded by circumstances beyond her control that she still refused to trust anyone.

Maggie wondered now if she'd underestimated

Noah. Would he have vouched for her character if she'd ignored the classified edict of the government and simply asked for his aid? Unfortunately, she knew she would never know the answer to that question.

TWO

She was hauntingly beautiful, more vulnerable than any woman he'd ever seen, and she reminded him of a wary doe who scented danger at every turn. It killed Noah to see Maggie this way, her confidence in tatters, her self-protective instincts like an impenetrable shield.

He remembered when she'd disappeared, her letters abruptly stopping and mutual friends shrugging when he'd asked about her. His initial assumption was that she'd gone into mourning. He hadn't allowed his dislike of Randall Hartley to prevent him from respecting her obvious need for privacy, but when the mail he periodically addressed to her via State continued to come back after two years marked Refused, he finally questioned those in authority. Their answers outraged him.

Noah concealed the resurging fury his

thoughts provoked, concentrating instead on Maggie—the woman he'd loved for as long as he could remember and despite the fact that another man had captured her heart before he'd recognized the depth of his own feelings for her.

Out of respect for Maggie, he'd kept his emotions to himself when she'd married Hartley, then his distance as the years unfolded. He loved her more deeply now, loved her with the seasoned maturity of a man who'd long ago abandoned the idea of finding her equal in any other woman. He'd hungered over the intervening years for the passion and sensuality lurking just beneath the poised image she reserved for strangers. He missed the emotional accessibility she'd always granted to her friends, just as he missed being the recipient of her thoughtful gestures, simple things like a tin of homemade cookies during the holiday season or an irreverent verse added to a birthday greeting. And he longed to reawaken her delight in the world around her and provide her with the kind of love that would always sustain her. She deserved to feel secure and happy again, and he was committed to becoming the man who helped her rediscover those feelings.

Holding her that morning had cost him dearly, but he hadn't been able to stop himself from touching her. She'd responded, shocking him, clearly shocking herself. He needed now to believe that she might want him, even if only out of loneliness. It no longer mattered to him why or how he attained a place in her life, because he wanted her and he intended to have her. All of her. Even the anguish etched into the fabric of her soul.

Noah hadn't rushed to her side the previous year, despite the impulse to do so when he'd learned the truth about her late husband and her subsequent banishment from the diplomatic community. Stunned by the machinations of those who'd deemed her disposable in the hallowed halls of global politics, he had used his power and prestige as a presidential advisor to obtain her location.

Noah monitored her daily routine through a private security firm, while simultaneously initiating a major change in his own professional life. The power brokers in Washington needed him far more than he needed them, and everybody involved knew it. He'd been planning his departure from State for a long time. He simply moved his plan up a few years.

Maggie, he sensed, would find it next to impossible to ever trust anyone in government again, especially after what she'd been through. He didn't blame her. Getting her to trust him would be tough enough, but he didn't intend to stop there, even though he knew he symbolized the powerful entity that had destroyed the life she'd once cherished. His plans for her were both far-reaching and complex. He expected her resistance, but he felt compelled to turn the tide, to help her reclaim her identity and her place in the world.

A savvy chess player since his youth and a negotiator of unparalleled skill, Noah Sutton grasped the complexity of the task ahead of him. He'd devoted time to planning his strategy, however, and he didn't intend to fail. Although he realized that Maggie already viewed him as a threat, he possessed the confidence unique to powerful men. He would triumph in the end.

"How long have you been in town?" Maggie asked once she finished the last bite of her raspberry-topped cheesecake.

Thank you, God, Noah thought with relief. He'd done most of the talking until now, entertaining her with anecdotes about the social customs of some of the more exotic nations he'd counseled in recent years. "Almost a week."

"You said you were on vacation." She took a sip of coffee, then placed the cup in the delicate china saucer.

Noting the tremor in her voice, he clenched his hands into fists and nodded. "For the most part."

She studied him for a moment, her gaze briefly flitting to his closed fists. Her remarkable blue eyes darkened a shade. "What's the other part?"

"Real estate in Carmel and Monterey."

"I've read that it's a buyer's market, especially for investment property."

He shook his head. "I'm looking for a home."

She stared.

"Even globe-trotters need a place to hang their hats."

"I'm surprised."

She wasn't surprised. She was stunned, and he knew it as well as he knew his own name. "Why be surprised? Everybody needs to feel rooted. I've waited a long time to select a permanent home and become a part of a community."

She pointed out, "Your roots are in New England. Vermont, to be precise. You have a large family there."

"My roots are where I choose to put them," he countered, his smile forced as he reached for his coffee. "I've sampled the world. This is where I want to live."

"Noah, I lost track of the times I heard you describe yourself as a contented vagabond. And your business is based in Zurich. Don't you have a home there?"

He chuckled dryly. "I have a penthouse in an overpriced five-star hotel. It's not much of a home. Are you really going to hold me to a remark I made more than ten years ago?"

"Of course not, but . . ."

"I'm an independent consultant. My loyalty is to myself and the people I employ. I can move the business, because I am the business."

"It's just that . . ."

"It's just that you're very protective of what you have here," he remarked, his usual finesse deserting him for a moment. "And you don't want anyone around who's going to remind you of the past. Close?"

"It doesn't matter to me where you live," she protested, her features growing more pale by the second. "Monterey's a sleepy little town, hardly a world capital. It's not at all the kind of place you're accustomed to, personally or professionally. You'll be bored in no time."

He looked around the restaurant. "These people don't look bored."

"Half of them are tourists, and you're twisting my meaning to suit yourself," she accused.

"Am I? I don't think so." He exhaled. "I thought it might matter. Our friendship, I mean."

She went very still. "We haven't seen each other in a long time, Noah."

"Six years," he reminded her for the second time that day.

"People change. Things happen that change them."

Her pointed remark didn't keep him from pressing a bit harder. "Your friends used to matter to you, Maggie-mine."

She gripped the arms of her chair, her temper flaring. "Don't call me that! And I don't have any . . ."

The arrival of their waiter, who freshened their coffee and asked again if they wanted anything from the bar, prompted her to leave her remark unfinished. Maggie looked away, pressing her fingertips to her temples.

Noah felt every bit of her stress as he watched her. He wanted to reassure her that she had nothing to fear from him, but instincts he trusted told him that this wasn't the time or the place.

"Friends?" he supplied in a low voice that only she could hear after their waiter departed. Noah struggled again with his anger at what had been done to her as she sucked in a gasp of dismay. He mastered the negative emotion before he spoke again. "You're wrong. I didn't relinquish your friendship when you disappeared three years ago, and I don't intend to now."

He watched through narrowed eyes as she settled back in her chair and composed herself. The first salvo had been fired, and he was betting on the strength that had fueled her survival in recent years to get them both through this first confrontation. Noah saw the price she paid for the control she exerted over herself, and it was all he could do not to apologize for backing her into a corner.

"Talk to me, Maggie-mine," he urged, ignoring her demand that he stop using the moniker he'd adopted for her early in their relationship. "I've never betrayed you. I don't plan to start now."

She shuddered, a flicker of hope flashing in her eyes before she blinked it away. "You'll be disappointed if you expect anything from me, Noah. The woman you once knew is gone. I buried her, along with my illusions, and she's not coming back."

"I can't accept that," he said quietly.

"You have no choice in the matter," she insisted. "No choice at all." She pushed up from her chair, her purse clutched between white-knuckled fingers, pride making her spine rigid enough to snap under the slightest pressure. "I need some fresh air. Then we'll deal with the issue we've been avoiding all evening. Once we do that, you can pack your bags and return to Zurich."

Noah watched her walk away as he reached for his wallet. Signaling their waiter, he calmed the worry that stole into his heart like a thief in the night and settled the bill. He'd expected their evening to be stressful, but that didn't mean he had to like it. Maggie had been forced to learn an array of survival skills in recent years. Her strength impressed him, but the reasons for it tore at him.

He found her not far from the front entrance of the restaurant. Counseling himself to proceed carefully with her, he paused a few feet from where she stood—an elegant, lonely woman who stared wistfully at the boat-cluttered bay. Noah contemplated her for a few moments, and the utterly bereft expression on her face made his heart shift painfully in his chest.

"I won't ever apologize for being honest with you, Maggie," he said quietly as he approached her.

She turned from the railing of the pier to look at him in the fading light of the balmy summer evening. Emotional fatigue shadowed her beautiful eyes, and wariness emanated from her. "And I won't apologize for who I am or how I feel."

"No one's asking you to do that."

"Then what do you want from me?"

He peered down at her. He wanted everything she had to offer, and then some, but he bit back the truth. She wasn't ready to hear it, so he modified his response. "The sound of your laughter, your compassion, your loyalty, and an end to this fear of betrayal that controls your life."

She flinched. "You're asking for a lot. More than I'm capable of."

"I don't believe that."

"Believe it, Noah, because it's the truth."

"The truth is that you're a survivor."

She shook her head, her denial mute but clear.

"You're also a casualty of other people's political agendas."

"I don't need reminders of reality."

"You remind yourself hourly, I suspect."

Maggie nodded, steely conviction in her voice as she spoke. "And I'll never stop reminding myself, because I can't afford to forget any of it. It's not going to happen again, Noah. Not ever."

He promised himself then that he would guard her from the users of the world until he breathed his last breath. Taking her hand, he tugged her away from the railing. "I ate too much. Why don't we stretch our legs while we talk?"

Looking startled by his suggestion and the fact that he'd taken her hand, she resisted for a split second and studied his face. He sensed she was searching for hidden motives, and he hated her wariness, almost as intensely as he hated the cause. Almost. He knew, too, that his multifaceted agenda would have scared the living hell out of her.

He smiled. "I don't bite." He'd spoken those words to her several times in the past, the most notable occasion when she'd come to his office that first time in Washington for an employment interview.

She flushed. "You're sure about that?"

He chuckled then, relief in the sound because he heard a hint of the old Maggie in her voice. He squeezed her slender fingers. Their palms met and mated. He felt her warmth, and it sent hunger spiraling through him. *Easy does it. She's fragile, and if you don't keep this light, you'll scare her into the next county.* "I've had all my shots."

"I certainly hope so," she parried back, a faint smile tugging at her lips. "All right then, let's walk."

"I like your dress. It suits you. Chanel?" The creamy silk was a classic. Hell, she was a classic and she did amazing things for the simple design, he amended silently.

Maggie darted an amused glance in his direction. "A very old Chanel. Probably a bona fide antique by now. I discovered it in a used clothing store in Paris several years ago."

"I thought I recognized it."

"You're an unusual man, Noah Sutton. Mr. Macho with a sensitive side."

He lazily arched a brow. "Was that a compliment?"

"Exactly."

He shrugged, his broad shoulders shifting beneath the custom fit of his suit jacket. "Comes from dating a bevy of runway models over the years, I expect."

"They trained you well."

Noah laughed. "I'll remember to add that to my resume."

"Sounds like a plan to me. Anybody special in your life these days?"

Oh, Maggie, you're so transparent. Compartmentalize me, and you'll feel safe. You're wrong, so incredibly wrong if you think I'll disappear politely this time around.

"My middle name is footloose. Considering my current lifestyle, it's probably best."

They paused and lingered at the end of the pier.

"I thought you'd be married by now," she said as she rested her forearms on the railing and watched the ball of orange on the horizon start to sink into the Pacific.

You were already taken. "Never found the right woman, I guess."

She sighed. "Look harder, Noah. The isolation wears on a person after a while."

"Sounds like good advice. Why haven't you

taken it?" he asked, aware as soon as the words left his mouth that he'd misstepped big time.

Maggie stared at him, then answered, "I can't, Noah. I just can't."

He silently cursed himself for spoiling her mood. Sliding his arm around her waist, he prayed that she wouldn't pull free of him as he tried to reassure her that he posed no threat to her emotional well-being. He felt her freeze, then draw in a breath before exhaling shakily. She didn't jerk back, though. Instead, she tentatively settled against him, the flaring curve of her hip and plumpness of her breast nudging against his side.

Billowing waves of heat invaded his body, a steamy brand of heat that inflamed his senses, thrummed in his veins, and tightened the muscles of his anatomy. He felt Maggie relax by degrees, her head coming to rest lightly against his shoulder. His body steadily hardened. Desire for her nearly swamped him, but he ruthlessly tamped down his physical response and allowed himself a moment of anticipation of the day when restraint wouldn't be necessary with her.

He craved the full force of her passion and an end to the fantasies she inspired. He craved the reality of pleasuring her to the edge of madness and then claiming her, gliding into her body, plunging deeply, repeatedly, until time stopped and nothing mattered but the two of them, their limbs tangled in passion as they aroused and satisfied each other. Over and over again. He craved this woman. He'd craved every facet of her for years.

"Let's get it over with," she said abruptly as she stepped free. She faced him, her shoulders squared, her expression a combination of resignation and determination to survive against the odds.

He knew exactly what she meant, so he didn't play games with her. "It's not necessary."

"Yes, it is, even though I promised myself I'd never speak of Randall or what he did to another living soul."

"I said it isn't necessary."

She gave him a disdain-filled look. "It's why you're here, Noah."

"No, it's not."

"Who sent you?"

Stunned, he just looked at her for a long moment before answering. "I've never been an errand boy, not even for heads of state."

"Other men have come to see me. They lacked your subtlety and style, and they certainly didn't take me out to dinner before they interrogated me, flashing their official identification and demanding answers to questions I didn't even understand."

Anger detonated within him. "No one sends me anywhere. Not ever!"

"It would be easier to believe you, but I don't."

His jaw tightened until it ached. Noah took a

moment to defuse his emotions. He disliked losing control. Even more, he disliked being called a liar, but he knew he couldn't let his temper speak for him. Right now he had to be satisfied with the belief that Maggie would eventually understand that his motives where she was concerned were honorable.

"Then don't believe me. That's your choice. As far as I'm concerned, you don't owe me or anyone else an explanation about Randall Hartley."

"You know, don't you? You know all of it."

He nodded, although he realized that he probably didn't know everything that had occurred. He had an excellent imagination, however, and he'd seen other cases like hers in his career. Too many, if the truth were told.

Maggie pressed her hands together, her fingers tangling as she waited for him to make the next move.

Her silence persisted. Noah reluctantly offered his opinion. "You were an innocent pawn in a high stakes game of political intrigue. You were used and then discarded. That's what I know, Maggie. It's the part I hate the most about the petty functionaries in the diplomatic world who destroy lives without a single thought to the consequences of their actions, all because they have some distorted vision of the greater glory inherent in political prominence. It's the reason I finally went into consulting. I couldn't tolerate those mindless idiots any longer. Hell! I won't tolerate them. They pervert the system."

Shocked, she searched his features, desperate to believe that he spoke the truth. So many people had turned their backs on her, abandoned her because they'd feared being tainted by any association with her. Others—those she didn't know—had simply terrorized her. Her innocence hadn't mattered. No one had even asked her if she'd been a party to the treasonous acts. The men who operated in the shadows behind the power brokers had assumed her guilt and treated her accordingly. Her reputation had been destroyed, her ability to work as a security-clearanced translator torn from her. She'd rebuilt from the ground up, lonely and fearful every step of the way that her life would be taken from her again.

Noah moved toward her. Maggie stiffened, ever mindful of his power and influence, not just the potential for an agenda that might jeopardize her. Oddly, though, she felt a mingling of relief and disappointment when he paused. She watched him extend his hand. She lifted her gaze to his face, her attention snagging on his strong features and the sincerity burning in the depths of his eyes.

Hope flirted with her. She wanted more than anything to believe that Noah believed in her. She wanted to trust him, as she'd once trusted him. She wanted the gift of his friendship. But why did he even care at all about a woman linked to the treason committed by her deceased husband?

Why would he risk his reputation? His reappearance in her life confused her. He had to have a motive, but she couldn't figure out what it was.

"Maggie, I know you were innocent."

Hope. It tempted her yet again. She whimpered, the distress-filled sound slipping past her lips before she could stop it. "Why do you know? How do you know?" she cried.

He swore, incredulity underscoring the crude word before he exclaimed, "For God's sake, I know you! The years that have passed don't matter. I know what you're made of, and I know that you have more integrity than any ten people either one of us could name right now."

"I want . . ." Fear clutched at her throat like razor-sharp talons, silencing her before she could complete the statement.

He took another step toward her. "Tell me what you want," Noah encouraged.

Held in thrall by the compassion in his eyes, she forced the words out. "What I've always wanted."

Tears brimmed in her eyes, the emotion rising up inside nearly choking her. She could feel herself unraveling inside, coming apart because the rigors of her lonely journey to survival had taken such a heavy toll. She needed to seize the glimmer of hope he offered, needed it more than anything right now.

"Tell me," he gently urged, closing the distance between them and curving his hands over her shoulders.

She felt his strength flow into her. She shuddered, then she found the courage to admit, "I wanted just one . . . just one . . . person to believe in me." Maggie lifted her face, her tears spilling free. She vaguely registered the pain that flashed in Noah's eyes as he stared down at her.

"Maggie . . ."

Her lower lip trembled before she sank her teeth into it to still the movement. She pulled in a tortured breath, fighting a losing battle for control. "Just one person, Noah. Just . . . one," she whispered as a ragged sob shook her. "But no one did. No one."

He embraced her then, stunning her with the fierceness of his hold on her once he gathered her against his muscular body. Shocking words, words of reassurance and support, poured out of him. She reeled like a drunk under the onslaught.

"Why didn't you contact me? Why didn't you let me help you? Didn't you know you could have trusted me? I've been worried sick about you. Dammit, Maggie, why?"

Dumbfounded, she had no answers for his questions. She felt too overwhelmed by this man who seemed to care so much, who seemed so blessedly sincere, who even seemed willing to shoulder some of the weight of the burden she'd carried alone for three excruciating years.

Something unexpected happened then, something that never would have occurred to her in a million years.

Maggie lifted her face from the curve of Noah's neck in the same instant that he drew back and looked down at her. She froze, almost drowning in the yearning that suddenly engulfed her as she stared up at him. His intense gaze told her that anything he had was hers if she wanted or needed it.

She wanted anything he had to offer, she realized. Anything. Everything.

She knew too well the depth of that need, because she'd guarded against it for so long. But her defenses tumbled when she saw the array of emotions blazing in Noah's eyes. Then she glimpsed smoldering desire, and it shocked her to her core.

A corresponding frisson of desire blossomed in her body, undulating into her bloodstream like hot honey. Desire, so acute that it nearly drove her to her knees, devastated the last vestiges of her resistance. She instinctively edged closer, burrowing against him, hungrier than she'd ever been in her entire life for emotional sustenance. She savored the strength of him. She even felt gratitude for the powerful body that sheltered her at that moment from the world.

She registered the heaviness of his loins a heartbeat later, but she didn't pull away. She sought even closer contact, wondering briefly if she'd lost her mind, then telling herself that it didn't matter.

She needed.

Dear God, how she needed.

Noah seemed to comprehend the depth of her need. Maggie didn't know how or why. She cared even less. She would accept what he offered for just a moment or two, she told herself as his mouth settled over hers, just long enough to feel something good again, just long enough to feel whole as a person and as a woman.

He tasted of cognac and coffee and desire. She adored the flavors. Parting her lips even more, she angled her head, granting and being granted greater access. She greedily drank in all that he offered, because she could think of nothing but saturating her senses with his unique taste.

He wasn't gentle. His touch was commanding, even forceful. Profoundly male. She rejoiced. Tenderness wasn't what she wanted right now. Too much finesse or the polished skill of an emotionally aloof man would have killed her trust in an instant.

She needed more. She needed to feel a man's heartbeat in his fingertips when he touched her.

She'd read once that kindness didn't always get the job done. She knew the truth of that observation, knew it better than most. Maggie wanted Noah's strength. She needed to be swept away. Not rescued, because she'd already been the architect of her own salvation. She simply wanted Noah to block out the world for her, if only for a little while.

Starved for emotional and physical intimacy, she trembled violently under the escalating force of their mingling desire. His arms tightened, his mouth fusing more tightly to her, his exploration of her so thorough that she grew dizzy. Noah's hunger seemed as overpowering and reckless as her own. That dazed realization rushed into her mind and departed just as quickly as he plundered her mouth and stroked her body.

Maggie didn't recognize him.

His possessiveness rocked her. She felt his touch everywhere. His hands seemed as frantic as her own had become—invading, discovering, molding, testing. He wasn't the self-contained, dispassionate diplomat she'd once known. Noah the Composed. Noah, the negotiator who'd become a legend in diplomatic circles because of his nerves of steel. She'd never known this side of him. Hot-blooded. Vibrating with sexual intent and sensuality. Voraciously hungry.

Maggie Holden no longer recognized herself, either.

She gasped at the heady feelings evoked by Noah's marauding mouth and hands. He murmured something vaguely reassuring. She surged against his sturdy frame, the building pressure of his loins and the intrusive thrust of his tongue a catalyst to her own insatiable hunger, a hunger that had already eclipsed the invisible boundary lines that had always tempered her passion.

She clutched at his shoulders, surrendering,

drowning happily, mindlessly in his desire until a hurtful memory pierced her consciousness. It momentarily stilled her racing heart and delivered simultaneous gut punches to her emotions and confidence.

Marriage had forced Maggie to learn passivity and compliance in bed. There had been less and less pleasure for her with each encounter. And then she'd learned about betrayal and the anguish that invariably followed.

Maggie died a little inside, her emotions shutting down, her fear of yet another betrayal returning, and her conviction that she'd just made a complete fool of herself almost suffocating her.

THREE

Noah felt her stiffen up on him just an instant before her emotional withdrawal began. He hated her need to distance herself from him, but he didn't fight the inevitability of Maggie's self-protective gesture.

He knew that things had gotten out of hand between them. Noah didn't regret it, though. He'd waited too many years for Maggie to feel a single moment of regret over a few minutes of shared intimacy with her.

"What are you trying to do to me?" she demanded in an unsteady voice.

How in hell was he supposed to answer a question like that? he wondered. He wasn't altogether sure how things had gotten to a flash point stage between them so quickly. He hadn't intended to kiss her, and he'd almost wound up making love to her on the pier.

"This is insane." She pushed at his hands and began to turn away. "You're insane if you think I'll ever let another man use me again."

He caught her before she completed her first step, his handling of her careful yet firm. "For God's sake, Maggie, don't run from me."

The illumination provided by lights strung along the pier revealed the panic and confusion in her eyes. An elderly couple strolled by just then, glancing curiously at them. Noah nodded in their direction, then returned his attention to the trembling woman who stood before him.

"I don't understand what you're trying to prove," she said in a low voice. "I'm not some blasted trophy. What is it about the men who run the world? Do you have some kind of contest going on at State to see who'll be the first in your crowd to sleep with Randall Hartley's widow?"

Shock lanced through him. A deathly stillness settled over his body, and his voice was tight with fury as he asked, "Who put that kind of pressure on you?"

Head bowed, she pressed her fingertips to her temples. Once she calmed herself, she lowered her hands to her sides and looked at him. "Go away, Noah. I'm begging you. Please let me have my memories of you. *They* don't hurt."

He demanded, "Who, Maggie?"

She shook her head, her stubborn nature much in evidence at that moment. "It's not important any longer."

The outrage he felt nearly overwhelmed him, but he got himself under control before his temper exploded. He'd deal with those responsible for her humiliation, in his own way and in his own time. For now, Noah focused on Maggie. "I'm not trying to prove anything," he said in response to her earlier question.

"Aren't you?" she asked.

"Do you want me to apologize for caring about you?"

Maggie stared up at him, stubbornness giving way to confusion.

"What exactly do you want?" he asked, his hands moving up and down her slender arms, caressing, reassuring, calming.

"What a question!" she exclaimed. "Too bad it doesn't ever get asked when it'll do some good."

"Tell me," he insisted, ignoring her outburst.

"I don't want anything, Noah, especially not sex. It doesn't solve anything."

He balked. He knew the difference between sex and love. He'd discovered it long ago, when it was too late to declare his feelings of love to Maggie and then satisfying only his physical needs with the women he'd known. His heart hadn't ever been truly nourished, and the absence of emotional substance in the relationships he'd had still haunted him.

Maggie made him feel. Emotions, desires, needs, hunger. The list seemed endless. No other woman had ever evoked such a litany of intensity within him.

"Nothing to say, Noah?" she pressed, her defenses like armed guards that had lined up around her.

"That wasn't sex."

"Then what was it?"

I love you. "I care about you, Maggie. I always have. Things got out of hand a few minutes ago. I didn't plan it. It just happened. Let it go."

She exhaled, the sound rife with disbelief and vulnerability.

He clenched his jaw for a moment. It was the only way he could control the devastation he felt. He reminded himself once again that she didn't understand that his emotions were like exposed nerve endings where she was concerned. If she realized the truth, he couldn't help wondering, would she still feel compelled to run from him? Disappointment reverberated within him, because he already knew the answer to his own question.

"Don't do this. What's between us got put on some damn back burner when you disappeared, I grant you, but it did not end then and you can't put a stop to it now."

Relenting somewhat, she said, "I'm trying to understand what just happened. I am also trying, without much success, to make you understand that I don't have anything left to give to a man, so please don't make this situation any more awkward than it already is."

"I'll accept whatever you can give," he said bluntly.

"Why won't you accept what I'm saying and just go away?"

"You're pushing me away because you're afraid. You have every right to be afraid after what you've been through, but I meant it when I said I'd never betray you."

She stared at him, her uncertainty evident.

"What do you want as proof?" he asked.

She seemed startled by his question. Although she searched his features in the dim light, she didn't answer him.

"What? Just tell me."

Her shoulders slumped under the pressure he exerted. "I don't know what I want," she confessed. "That's not true. I know that I don't want to be used again. I wouldn't survive it, Noah." She fingered her lower lip, which was still damp and swollen from his kisses. "That shouldn't have happened. It can't happen again."

He inclined his head, but he said nothing. What could he say when his body still burned with desire and his heart ached for her?

"I don't know you," she said.

He understood precisely what she meant. "You know me, Maggie."

"Not when you're . . ." She paused, color staining her cheeks.

He grimly filled in the blank space she left. "Not when I feel passion or desire . . . for you?"

She nodded. "You've never behaved that way around me. I never saw that side of you, not even when you were with other women. You've always been so in control. You've changed, Noah," she said, accusation in her voice.

He might have laughed at her consternation with him under any other circumstances. "So you'll exact a penalty because I responded to you? What will that accomplish? Be honest. Until you pushed me away, you wanted me as much as I wanted you. You can pretend to yourself that you didn't feel anything if you must, but don't lie to me. I don't deserve that from you."

She exhaled. "I cannot deal with this situation right now."

Her distress prompted him to say, "Then we'll deal with it tomorrow."

She shivered suddenly and looked away. Noah didn't draw her into his arms to shelter her from the breeze blowing in off the bay, despite the urge to do so. He knew he'd already pushed her to the limits of her emotional tolerance.

"You're getting chilled. Let's get you home."

Maggie didn't meet his gaze. "Please," she whispered.

They made their way down the length of the pier, side by side but miles apart as they walked to his rental car. The silence between them persisted as he drove the short distance to her home.

Noah parked in front of the cottage, but he made no move to get out of the vehicle. He watched Maggie, saw the strain of the evening in the way she fiddled with the shoulder strap of her purse and stared out the front window of the car.

"How did you find me?" she finally asked.

"Peterson, although he wasn't too thrilled about it."

She flinched. "The head of security at State. A truly sensitive and compassionate man."

He didn't acknowledge her sarcasm. Peterson was a single-minded and very zealous bureaucrat. Nothing further needed to be said about him, but Noah had plenty to say to him. His people had violated the laws of decency and the land.

"I'm surprised you bothered. Knowing me certainly won't enhance your reputation in diplomatic circles."

"Did you expect *all* of your friends to abandon you?"

"They did." Her voice was flat.

"Not all," he insisted. "You should be bitter, but the only emotion I hear in your voice is resignation."

"Bitterness is a waste of time and energy." She laughed hollowly.

Noah instinctively started to reach out to her, but stopped. The restraint he exercised taking all the self-control he possessed.

Pushing open his door, Noah walked around to her side of the car. She got out, brushed past him, and made her way to the front porch of her small cottage.

Noah followed her, pausing at the foot of the stairs and watching as she dug around in her purse for her keys. He waited while she shoved the key into the lock, then nudged the front door open.

Turning to face him, she said, "Please don't come back, Noah, for both our sakes."

"Does everyone have to have a motive?"

Her eyes filled with tears. She jerked a nod in his direction. "Unfortunately, that's been my experience."

Noah swore, the harsh word reflecting the tumult of emotions coursing through him at that moment. Unable to keep himself away from her any longer, he climbed the stairs and crossed the shallow porch. He paused next to her, aware that her uneasiness had returned when he saw the look in her eyes. Reaching past her, he found the switch on the inside wall and extinguished the porch light glaring brightly over their heads.

Noah trusted his instincts in the minutes that followed. He drew Maggie forward and simply held her, his sole motive to comfort her. She was rigid at first, like a slim wedge of granite, but then she sighed, sagged against him, and trembled with emotion. Noah fought the arousal her shapely body caused, fought it with every bit of inner strength he possessed.

It took several minutes, but he felt some of the tension in her ease as she stood within the circle of his arms. Sliding her arms around his waist, she rested her cheek against his shoulder. He savored the moment and the fledgling quality of her trust.

"I must seem so frightened to you," she finally said.

Noah pressed a kiss to the top of her fair head. "With good reason."

"Are you serious about buying real estate in Carmel or Monterey?"

"Absolutely."

"I really am surprised."

"I'm tired of the high visibility lifestyle. I want something a bit more relaxed now."

"You always seemed to like having a high profile in the diplomatic community."

"I did, especially in the early years, but after a while it was nothing more than a part of the job I had to do."

"Then it's not an ego thing with you?" she asked.

"Periodically, I suppose it was. Maybe it still is. I work hard, and I've helped put several third world countries on the map economically. I'm proud of what I've accomplished, and I don't mind taking credit. When you're dealing with heads of state, you're always dealing with their fragile egos too. Human nature is painfully predictable at times."

She laughed softly. "You sound terribly jaded."

He shrugged. "I am about some things. It goes with the territory."

"You wield a great deal of power."

"Don't let it bother you. I don't take it all that seriously any longer."

She looked up at him. "I don't want to be overwhelmed, Noah. I won't have some meaningless affair. I couldn't handle the aftermath."

He cupped her face between his broad-palmed hands and peered down at her. "I don't have meaningless affairs. I don't like the way I feel when they're over. I learned that a long time ago. A very long time ago. Besides, I meant it when I said I wouldn't ask anything of you beyond what you can give. You have boundary lines based on the experiences you've had, and I'll respect them."

"How long will you be here?"

The moon cast streamers of light across her upturned face. He studied her for several moments, his reply reminiscent of a vow when he answered her. "As long as it takes, Maggie-mine. As long as it takes. I've waited too many years for a sense of contentment and some genuine happiness."

She managed a tentative smile. "There are some lovely homes here."

Not bothering to correct her, he nodded. Noah knew she didn't completely believe his story that a real estate acquisition was the primary objective of his presence in the area, but he kept his awareness to himself. He knew, too, that she would remain wary and guarded. He dealt with his conscience by reminding it that he planned to tell Maggie the whole truth as soon as he felt he could risk it. Until then, he knew he needed to bide his time and regain her trust, not just seduce her back into the world that had very nearly destroyed her. In the final analysis, Maggie was essential to the partnership he envisioned, although she didn't know it yet.

"The realtors I've dealt with this past week are good," he remarked. "I've seen several possibilities that I like, but I could use a female perspective I trust. How about it?"

Maggie's surprise showed. "Me? Why? You're looking at estates. I live in a small cottage. Our tastes and budgets are poles apart."

He tapped the tip of her nose with his finger. "Yes, you, and the reason should be obvious. You've always known how to turn a house into a home. I'd like to know if you see any real potential in these places."

"If you're sure." She sounded dubious. "When and where shall I meet you?"

He scowled at her. "I'll pick you up in the morning."

"Not before ten. I don't use alarm clocks when I'm on vacation."

"Ten sharp."

He turned to leave, even though he longed to stay. He let his common sense guide him down the stairs to the sidewalk, even though his body still ached painfully. He feared that ache would be a part of his reality for quite some time, but he decided to endure it. Too much was at stake not to.

'Noah?"

He glanced back at her. Maggie stood in the shadow-darkened doorway, the pale silk of her dress and her paler hair giving her an incandescent look. In order to ease his flaring desire, he groused, "All right. Ten-thirty, but that's the latest."

She shook her head. "Ten's fine." She paused, then asked, "Do you remember that I always knew when you were being a diplomat and when you were being a person?"

He smiled. "I remember everything, Maggie. Get a good night's sleep."

He waved and got into his rental car, then waited as she stepped into her home and secured the front door. Noah started the car and eased onto the deserted side street. He'd heard another echo of the old Maggie when she'd questioned him, and he liked the sound. He chuckled as he drove to his hotel, aware that she'd ever so politely called him a liar. This one time, he didn't mind. He didn't mind at all, because he viewed her remark as a sign that he'd briefly lured her out of her self-imposed prison.

Maggie slowly made her way through her cottage, turning off lights and glancing at each window she passed to make certain it was closed and locked.

She didn't bother with the lamp on the night table once she entered her bedroom. The shaft of moonlight that pierced the sheer curtains covering the window above her bureau provided sufficient illumination. She undressed in the semidarkness of the room, donned a simple ankle-length cotton nightgown, and climbed into bed.

She didn't expect to fall asleep right away. She knew in her heart that her thoughts of Noah and the emotional turmoil he'd caused made any quest for sleep virtually useless.

Noah tempted her. Tempted her in ways that shocked and unnerved her. He reminded her of needs long suppressed, needs beyond the physical, soul-deep, heart-wrenching needs never fulfilled. He also made her feel like an emotional coward, and she resented it. Her survival in recent years had depended solely on her. Trust wasn't possible for her any longer, because to trust meant making herself vulnerable.

Noah posed other risks, as well. Attractive, intelligent, and altogether too sophisticated for his own good, he reminded her of enticing but very forbidden fruit. He'd stunned her with the volatile quality of his passion. Her senses still reeled from the desire she'd experienced in his embrace. No man had ever affected her so profoundly or made her so hungry for shared intimacy.

Maggie surrendered herself to her memories of Noah, because not to do so smacked of fighting the inevitable. She'd learned in the aftermath of

Randall's treason and murder to confront her emotions and resolve them privately. She wasn't always successful, but she tried to be honest with herself.

She recalled then the years she'd spent as Noah's personal translator at the State Department. The daughter of academics, she'd grown up on a series of college campuses and enjoyed the protected life of an only child. Her arrival in Washington had been a chance thing—the result of an invitation from friends of her parents to interview for a position as a translator.

She'd come armed with her language skills, her innocence, an ability to laugh at herself, and an eagerness to embrace and experience the world. The actual interview had turned into three meetings with Noah. He'd behaved like a dictator each time, deliberately testing her mettle, he'd later confessed.

She and Noah traveled the globe together at a breakneck pace, working as a team, communicating with their own special language whenever his negotiations reached a critical stage, celebrating his triumphs, and periodically commiserating over his few failed attempts to bring economic stability to a particular region of the world. He'd trusted her with his professional concerns, protected her from inebriated politicos, and stood at her side when she'd buried her parents following a freak car accident in upstate New York.

Together they had sampled a hundred different cultures, dined on exotic, and some downright awful, cuisines, shopped colorful bazaars in search of mementos of their trips, and even dodged bullets together in outposts that were still to this day strife torn. As they'd jetted around the world, she'd experienced Noah's impatience with people in the diplomatic community who'd lacked his vision and insight. She'd shared his contempt when he'd dealt with pettiness, seen his generosity with people who needed medical care, and felt the force of his anger when he encountered injustice. She'd laughed at his silly jokes. She'd been the beneficiary of his kindness and compassion when she'd suffered a nearly terminal bout of food poisoning during a trip to Moscow, then returned the favor a month later when they were stranded in an Eastern European backwater that had no doctor.

They had a history. A history that she now realized she'd relinquished somewhat grudgingly at the time of her marriage, and then once again when she'd walked away from the diplomatic community.

Maggie sighed. Noah Sutton. He could be a charmer, a despot, or a choirboy, depending upon his mood. She smiled. Sometimes even all three simultaneously.

Now, she knew of his ability to seduce. The shock of that discovery still echoed within her, like church bells pealing discordantly. Thoroughly unnerved by what they'd shared earlier that evening, she feared that her senses would never calm themselves and that the hunger she now felt would never be satisfied. The potential for betrayal still haunted her, prevented her from giving herself to any man, she knew, and she refused to apologize for her apprehension.

She suddenly remembered Noah's women. His reputation as a playboy had been cemented by a bevy of beauties. Women who reminded Maggie of trophies, women who in turn considered Noah a trophy because of his power and influence. A world-famous diva, numerous models, a countess with a penchant for diamonds the size of walnuts, a bona fide Middle Eastern princess with a wretched temper. There were too many in his past to itemize, so she didn't even try.

Maggie suspected, though, that those women symbolized the sole character flaw in the man. He never committed long-term. His affairs were short, despite the best efforts of the various women involved. Maggie had often wondered why during the early years of their working relationship, and she'd finally concluded that he had a genuine aversion to emotional intimacy, not just a short attention span.

Even after she'd married and settled into her new life as the wife of a diplomat on the rise, rumors about Noah's women continued. She heard them all, because diplomatic circles were small and gossip was a pastime that most people engaged in when they socialized. She saw him infrequently after marrying. She missed him, though, and when their paths crossed she always took the opportunity to reminisce about the adventures they'd shared.

Maggie stared into the darkness as a ragged sob ripped through her, then another. So much had gone wrong, so much she still didn't understand.

How, she asked herself for the thousandth time, could she have been so thoroughly misjudged by everyone? How?

As always, her questions remained unanswered. Maggie tiredly brushed at the tears that slipped down her cheeks just as one thought pierced through the haze of her emotional fatigue. *Noah*. If there was one man she could still believe in, it would be Noah.

and when that path crossed she always took the opportunity to reminisce about the adventures they'd shared.

Maggie searched [illegible] a ragged [illegible] So much [illegible] understood.

How she asked herself for the thousandth time, could she have been so completely mistaken in [illegible]?

As [illegible] her [illegible] Maggie [illegible] of the [illegible] dropped down her cheeks and [illegible] filtered through the [illegible] of her [illegible] Yet [illegible] she could still believe in [illegible] Nash.

FOUR

Maggie slept restlessly that night. Her dreams resembled an erotic torture chamber, replete with sensual images that left her shaking with desire for Noah. Those tantalizing images, and the hunger they induced, eventually drove her from her bed shortly before dawn.

Determined to regain control over herself, Maggie brewed a pot of tea, checked the front porch to make certain that Noah wasn't out there reading her Sunday paper before she retrieved it, and adjourned to the sunroom at the rear of the cottage. Everything she read, from the headlines touting a new United Nations peace accord between warring factions in the Middle East to the latest antics of a well-known and very temperamental San Francisco opera star, seemed destined to remind her of Noah.

She shoved the newspaper aside in frustration,

changed into gardening clothes, and went outside to attend to her roses. She vengefully pounced on every weed she spotted, yanking them out of the ground by the roots and tossing them into the tin bucket she kept at her side as she methodically moved up and down the rows of colorful rosebushes.

Despite her best efforts, nothing she did kept her thoughts from straying back to Noah. She gave up the battle against the sensual fantasies that streamed through her mind at about the same time that she abandoned her weed patrol. After depositing her soiled clothes in the laundry hamper and donning a caftan, she fixed a light breakfast and read the newspaper in earnest.

Noah continued to stroll through her mind as the morning unfolded, even while she bathed and dressed for their day together. Still very unsettled by his impact on her, Maggie grudgingly accepted her desire for Noah as a reality she needed to cope with. She also let herself hope that he was as sincere as he seemed.

What could it hurt to hope a little? she asked herself. It could hurt a whole lot, a voice in her head repeatedly cautioned.

Maggie managed to summon a surface calm shortly before Noah's arrival. As she opened the front door, she greeted him by remarking, "I could always set a clock by your punctual nature."

Looking far too ruggedly appealing for her fragile emotional state, he smiled at her, but his smile faded almost immediately. "Didn't you get any sleep last night?"

She frowned. "Thanks. You look wonderful too."

Noah stopped her march across the front porch after she jerked the front door closed and pocketed her keys. "What's the matter?"

Her poise departed like a crowd fleeing a fire-ravaged building. "*You're* the matter," she blurted out, then regretted even opening her mouth.

Taking her by the hand, Noah led her to a wicker chair on the porch and gently forced her to sit down. He settled into the chair opposite her, his long legs stretched out in front of him, his gaze sharp as he perused her features.

Maggie sat perched on the edge of her seat, her tension obvious. She refused to meet his gaze, staring instead at a patch of peeling paint on the wall just beyond his right shoulder.

"Talk to me. We're not going anywhere until you do."

She sighed. Annoyed with herself, she squared her shoulders and gave him a direct look. "I'd rather not, if you don't mind."

"Maggie . . ." he gently coaxed.

"I can't, Noah. My thoughts are in a tangle. I couldn't articulate them right now if my life depended on it."

"Have I made you that uncomfortable?" he asked.

"You don't make me uncomfortable," she insisted. Yes, he does, her conscience screeched.

"Then, what?"

"I'm just a little edgy."

"Did you sleep at all?"

"For a while."

"Maggie, I'm trying to make a new life for myself. Nothing more," he said quietly.

She nodded.

"So try to relax. I wouldn't harm you for the world."

She studied him, but she said nothing. She wanted so desperately to take him at his word, but fear stalked her, crippled her ability to believe in anyone, even Noah. She felt ashamed, but she didn't know how to dismiss the impulse to remain vigilant.

"You can believe me. I've never lied to you."

"You make it sound so simple, but nothing in my life has been even remotely simple for several years."

"Then it's about time to change that pattern, isn't it?"

"I obviously have a major problem with trust, Noah."

"With good reason, but try to put aside your suspicions where I'm concerned. You won't regret it, I promise."

She nearly smiled. "Who's talking right now? Noah the Man or Noah the Negotiator, the diplomatic envoy who's capable of charming an agreement out of the devil himself?"

His expression sobered. "The man, Maggie. Only the man. I'm here for myself. No one else."

"I really want to believe you."

"I'd be happy with a sincere attempt right now."

Standing, he extended his hand. Maggie hesitated. She looked up at him, searching his face for any hint that he was lying or laying the groundwork to orchestrate some horrific catastrophe that would end with Maggie Holden being stripped of her identity again. She found no such hint, however, only compassion and understanding in his rugged features and steady gaze. Aware that she'd instantly assumed the worst, she felt chagrined with herself. Noah was right, she concluded. She needed to get past the fear that had become her yardstick for everything and everyone.

Maggie slowly got to her feet, silently resolving that she would find a way to move beyond her fear of history repeating itself. She reached out to accept Noah's hand. A current of warmth stole into her senses the instant their palms connected. His hand engulfed hers, his fingers weaving through her slender ones. His touch the night before had shredded her defenses, left her shattered and shaking with desire. Now, his secure hold felt like a lifeline, not just a reminder of his physical strength and his sensuality.

As she peered up at Noah, she couldn't stop

the questions that darted into her head, though. Why did he have to be the one to arouse her sensual needs and the hunger for emotional closeness that thrived within her? Why hadn't he kept his hands to himself?

Why couldn't life be simple?

Then a completely different kind of question sneaked into her head. What harm could there be in sharing a day or two with Noah? None, she firmly told herself. Absolutely none. After all, she was an adult, and she could control herself and her urges.

"Smile for me."

She did, but almost shyly.

"Let's forget about everyone and everything but ourselves today, all right?"

"That would be wonderful."

"And you'll put yourself in my capable hands?"

"I'll try," she promised, refusing to back away from the commitment she'd just made to relax and enjoy herself.

"That's a start," Noah said. "Come here, Maggie-mine."

He drew her against his hard body, holding her for several moments. It was a little like being reeled into the center of an overstoked furnace. There was nothing overtly sexual about Noah's embrace, but she felt his heat and virility penetrate her skin and saturate her bones almost immediately. Her pulse picked up speed, and she fought the urge to curl into him and surrender every part of herself.

A moment later Maggie experienced a shocking discovery. She found not just desire but emotional sustenance, too, in Noah's arms.

She told herself that feeling might be safe with Noah, as long as she protected her heart and engaged her common sense whenever they were together. She prayed she had the strength to do both.

"Let's get this show on the road," he said as he released her. "We've got a lot to do today."

Maggie smiled at the familiar words. They tripped some kind of mental switch in the recesses of her mind, transporting her back to a happier time, a time of laughter, whirlwind travel schedules, and constant challenges. "Your wish is my command," she quipped, her remark an echo of past irreverence when he'd behaved like an autocratic general assembling his troops.

"If you call me Fearless Leader, I'll paddle your fanny," he warned.

Feeling suddenly carefree, she grinned at his threat as she darted away from him and down the porch steps. "Fearless Leader!" she called out over her shoulder. "Catch me if you can."

"Watch and see if I don't," he said softly enough not to be heard as he followed her to the car. "Just watch and see."

As Maggie wandered aimlessly along the beach after they'd satisfied their hunger with the contents of the picnic lunch basket he'd had packed that morning at his hotel, Noah grappled with the steadily escalating arousal that tightened his muscular body into knots and flooded his bloodstream with scorching heat. He wondered wryly as he watched her if anyone had ever died from the condition he was in. It was a grim thing to ponder, so he dismissed the thought.

Maggie paused to inspect a shell on the beach, and Noah recalled the enormous crystal bowl she'd once kept in the center of her dining room table in Rome. Filled with unique shells that she'd gathered in her travels across the world, the container had always reminded Noah of her sentimental nature. He'd enjoyed listening to her regale her guests with humor-filled anecdotes about the exact locations in which she'd discovered each of her treasures, as she'd called them.

Over the years, Noah had come to realize that Maggie hadn't ever been a collector of photos to mark the events or places of her life; instead, she'd collected memories in the form of chipped seashells. Noah wished he'd understood the reason for her behavior in those days. He felt certain he did now, however, and it pained him to realize how lonely she must have been in her marriage.

Maggie straightened suddenly and headed back to the picnic table situated on a low bluff that overlooked the beach. Empty-handed, she settled on the bench beside Noah. She smiled at him as she dusted the sand from her feet and slid them into her deck shoes.

"None worth keeping?" he asked, referring to the shells he'd watched her inspect for the last twenty minutes.

She shook her head. "I don't collect them anymore. Transplanting them seems unfair."

He nodded, aware that she spoke of herself, not simply of the litter the sea had deposited on the northern California shoreline. He kept his gaze on the ocean swells slapping against the rock formations that jutted out of the water a few hundred yards from shore. Scores of bulky-looking sea lions lolled on the ancient volcanic extrusions, barking and squealing at one another. A vast array of birds indigenous to the area glided and swooped overhead in patterns graceful enough to make a skilled barnstormer envious, and otters alternately frolicked atop the waves and scavenged the floating seaweed just below the surface of the Pacific.

"Why Monterey?" Noah finally asked.

Drawing her legs up, Maggie looped her arms around her upraised knees. "My parents brought me here for summer vacations during the years they taught at Berkeley. The good memories I had of the area surfaced when things started unraveling in my marriage, and then again after Randall died." Looking pale, Maggie cast a sidelong glance in his direction, then quietly admitted, "I felt safe here when I was a child, so I decided to come back. End of story."

"Do you? Feel safe, I mean."

She nodded. "Most of the time. No place is perfect, of course, but I like teaching at the academy. And now I have a real home and enough space for my roses."

Noah leaned back against the edge of the tabletop. "I've never felt connected to a piece of real estate."

Maggie smiled faintly. "How could you? You're never anywhere long enough to settle in. Besides, I'm starting to think that the only really important connection in life has to do with peace of mind."

"What about people, Maggie?"

She answered him with the kind of candor that possessed the power to surprise and dismay. "I'm not the right person to answer that question, Noah. I'm not close to anyone any longer."

"By choice, I assume."

She tensed. "It wasn't my choice, and you know it. I'm just dealing with the results of the choices that other people made for me three years ago."

He forged on, ignoring her defensiveness. "Monterey represents a place of recovery, then, not just a haven."

"Yes, it does."

"How recovered are you, Maggie? Do you

want your life back, or are you going to stand on the sidelines and watch the world go by?"

"Why are you asking me these questions?"

He seized her hand, preventing her departure when she started to get up. She sank back down beside him, her wariness evident as she waited for his reply.

"Not out of idle curiosity, I assure you."

Maggie stared at him.

"If I don't understand the woman you've become, how can I be a good friend?"

She looked away. Lifting her hands, she brought her fingertips to her temples. Noah simply watched her, aware that he couldn't fight her battles for her, not if she had any hope of winning her personal war against fear and apprehension. He was committed to helping her discover that she had the strength to reclaim her identity. Only then, he realized, would they have a chance to enjoy the life he wanted to share with her.

When she finally lowered her hands, she muttered, "I'm cautious." Tears brimmed in her large eyes. "I hate being this way, feeling this way."

He squeezed her fingers. "We'll get you through it, I promise. Now, tell me about your relationships with the people at the academy."

"There's not much to tell, Doctor. We're acquainted because of what we do, but that's all."

Good girl, he thought, proud that her instinctive humor was struggling to reemerge. "Don't you want more?"

She sighed, the soft sound snatched away almost immediately by the unseasonably warm June breeze. "I need my privacy, Noah, but I'm not a total recluse all of the time. I attend school functions. I even wander up to San Francisco every now and again to shop and attend the ballet." She smiled, a glimpse of the old Maggie in her expressive facial features. "They have a wonderful company of dancers."

"I remember how much you enjoyed that kind of thing in Europe."

"Yes, I did."

Noah shifted mental gears. "I went home to Vermont last Christmas. I even considered living there for a while."

"What made you decide against it?"

"A twenty-year absence."

She nodded sagely, then observed, "Life goes on, whether or not you're a part of it."

"Something like that," he agreed. "My brothers have the company well in hand now that Dad's retired. They seemed uncomfortable with my suggestions for expanding the business during the one board meeting I attended, so I signed over my proxy and politely departed."

"I'm still surprised."

"By what?"

"That you'd give up so easily, especially if you wanted to be a part of things."

"I didn't, and I don't. I wanted to help, but I

quickly realized that I was just going through the motions."

She peered at him, a slight frown wrinkling her brow. "You've changed, haven't you?"

He shrugged. "Maybe. Probably."

"You have changed, Noah. Take my word for it."

He took her hand, clasping it between his two larger ones. "Life's fluid. Isn't that what you once told me?"

She smiled. "I was extremely profound in the old days, wasn't I?"

"You still are, and you haven't lost your fresh mouth, either."

She arched an elegant brow. "Did you expect me to?"

"I was hoping you hadn't. You're the only woman I've ever known who's totally honest. It's a quality I appreciate, even if it's ego deflating at times."

"You've always had an enormous ego, so I don't think you're in much danger from my mouth."

I just want another taste of it. Noah groaned silently as he looked back at her. He wanted her so badly that his insides shook at the thought of possessing her. He wondered, because he couldn't dispel the worry he felt, if she would ever unbend enough to trust him. Without that foundation, he knew they were destined for failure. The restraint he exercised in the moments that followed took a toll on him, but he knew not doing so would have meant giving in to impulses that would have jeopardized the progress they were making.

"You have an odd look on your face," Maggie said.

He almost laughed, would have laughed if the longing he felt hadn't settled so deeply into his bones. "Just thinking."

"About what?"

"The estate we looked at before lunch," he managed as he pressed a kiss to the back of her hand and then released her.

"It's as big as a museum and just about as inviting."

"My thoughts exactly."

"How many more are we going to look at today?"

"Four, I think."

She glanced at her watch as she pushed up from the bench. "It's after two. Maybe we should get started."

Noah stood as well, the desire still hammering at his insides almost crippling. He reached for the picnic basket. Maggie reached for it in the same instant. Their hands met above the basket's handle. Noah grimaced.

Maggie glanced at him. "Problem?"

Noah shook his head, feeling foolish and juvenile.

She withdrew her hand. "Noah, what's wrong?"

The armor around his heart cracked. He felt it happening, and the words that spilled past his lips would have embarrassed him if anyone but this woman had heard them. "I want a real home, Maggie-mine."

She stepped toward him. Noah sensed that she was responding instinctively. That's how he remembered her, before the humiliation and betrayal she'd been forced to endure. That openhearted quality was one of many that he'd always loved about her. She slipped into his arms, hugging him tightly once she slid her arms around his waist. She offered the kind of reassurance that was typically Maggie. She unknowingly tantalized him, too, the swell of her breasts plumping against his chest, the natural cradle of her upper thighs fitting intimately against his loins and setting him aflame. He shuddered as he held her close, then cautioned himself not to frighten her.

Maggie gently extricated herself from his embrace a few moments later. "You've gotten lonely over the years, haven't you?"

He spoke with an intensity that reflected the emptiness that had become a permanent resident in his heart. "Yeah, I guess I have."

"You won't be lonely here."

He smiled to cover the emotional and physical strain that seemed destined to overwhelm him when they were together. "Promise?" he said, struggling to tease, to lighten the moment before she read the truth of his feelings for her in his eyes.

"I promise, Noah." She hesitated, then whispered, "I'm glad you're here. I've missed you."

FIVE

"You're smiling," Noah remarked. "It's the first time since we left the beach."

Maggie cast an amused glance in his direction as they walked through the sprawling twenty-room house, the last property on their afternoon tour, but she refrained from speaking. The estate, which comprised just under three acres at the edge of the Pacific in Carmel, reminded her of the country homes that she'd visited many years ago in the south of France. She had a genuine fondness for the gracious but relaxed architectural style typical of the region.

They ended their inspection of the main house in the kitchen, a spaciously designed and equipped area that would have warmed the heart of any chef. An entire wall of glass opposite the kitchen provided a panoramic view of carefully tended gardens situated just beyond the rear terrace.

Maggie paused in the center of the room, her smile widening even more.

"The suspense is killing me."

She met his gaze. "This is the best of the lot, Noah. This place has the potential of being turned into a real home."

"You like it?"

She laughed at his understatement. "I don't just like it. I love it."

"Reminds you a little of the south of France, doesn't it?"

Maggie nodded, not at all surprised by his memory of her appreciation for certain styles of architecture. She'd already discovered during their day together that Noah remembered many things that she'd long ago surrendered to the past. She noticed an ice bucket that had been left in the center of the breakfast table on the opposite side of the room. A bottle of what appeared to be champagne sat up to its neck in chipped ice. Two crystal goblets stood beside the silver bucket.

"Someone's planning a celebration."

"Mr. Sutton?" a female voice called out before Noah responded to Maggie's observation.

"Be right with you, Mrs. Farley." To Maggie, he said, "She's the realtor who's handling the property. I'll be back in a few minutes. Why don't you take a look at the garden?"

Maggie nodded. She made her way out onto the terrace and down the flagstone steps to the garden while Noah located the realtor. She wandered along the meandering pathway. Surrounded by every possible manner of fragrant floral offering, including a vast array of roses, her senses and her imagination were captivated by the lush beauty of the well-planned garden. She envied Noah the option of owning so much land.

He was true to his word. He walked out onto the terrace less than five minutes later, carrying two champagne-filled goblets.

Maggie met him at the top of the terrace steps, her smile relaxed, her eyes alight with curiosity. "What are you celebrating?"

"We're celebrating the purchase of a home," he said as he handed her a goblet.

Momentarily horrified by his impulsiveness, Maggie stared at him. "Just like that? You bought it?"

He smiled at her. "Why are you so surprised?"

"I shouldn't be, should I? You were never one to march to anyone's drummer but your own."

His expression sobered. "I told you I wanted a real home, and I wasn't kidding when I said I was tired of five-star hotels and not feeling rooted."

She nodded slowly, still a little overwhelmed by his decisiveness. "I believe you, Noah."

"My staff's already closing up the office in Zurich, and my household goods are in transit even as we speak."

Not certain what to say, Maggie sipped her champagne and walked to the edge of the terrace.

"Penny," he said as he stood behind her.

"It's nothing." *It* was a sensation of uneasiness that had just crept over her with the stealth of a cat burglar.

"You were right all along, you know. I do have more than one reason for deciding to move here."

She simply turned and looked up at him, all her doubts visible in her enormous blue eyes and her vulnerable facial expression.

"I'm not planning to turn this place into a mecca for foreign dignitaries, so put your mind at ease."

"That's hard to do, since you're a part of that world. It's what you do."

"It's not what I am, though. Hasn't that occurred to you yet?"

"What's just occurred to me is that you're a very clever man. You can be single-minded to the point of ruthlessness when a situation calls for that kind of behavior, and you also have the ability to simultaneously juggle several agendas, both personal and professional."

"You have an excellent memory," he said mildly, his expression unreadable.

"Yes, I do. I don't like games, Noah."

"This isn't a game."

"Isn't it?"

"No."

"I won't be manipulated."

He appeared unperturbed by her flashing temper, which simply added to her frustration. She pushed past him, depositing her champagne goblet on a patio table as she made her way to the French doors that led into the kitchen.

"Maggie," he said sharply.

Something in his voice made her hesitate, made her turn and look at him. She heard urgency, and something more, but she couldn't define the something more. His facial expression remained implacable, hard lines and angles that revealed nothing.

She'd seen him this way more times than she could count, the ultimate chess player during international trade negotiations. Noah made his moves with finesse and great calculation. He always had. She'd understood the need in his role as a representative of their government, but the need ended, as far as she was concerned, in personal relationships. She suddenly felt maneuvered into a corner, and she loathed the feeling. Absolutely loathed it.

"Don't make the mistake of treating me like one of your pawns."

"This isn't a chess game, Maggie-mine."

Despite his deadly serious tone of voice, she said, "No, it's my life, and nobody gets to tamper with it. Not even you."

"Then think of this situation as a puzzle, and you're the only one qualified to assemble the pieces on the board."

"Say what you really mean, Noah," she challenged.

"I just did."

He approached her, towering over her just moments later and blocking out the afternoon sun as he peered down at her. She stared at him. Uncertainty that threatened to turn into full-fledged panic flirted with the control she exercised over herself.

"What are you thinking right now?" he asked.

"That I may be cautious, but I'm not stupid."

He nodded, as though agreeing with her, but he offered her nothing in the way of reassurance to ease the trepidation she felt. Anger replaced all the other emotions threatening her at that moment. Her eyes darkened with it, and she unknowingly clenched her hands into fists at her sides.

"I don't deserve your anger," he said, his tone infuriatingly calm.

"I think you do."

"Have I ever hurt you?"

That question stopped her reeling emotions in midspin. He hadn't. That was the truth. Noah had never hurt her. He'd been dictatorial, self-absorbed, impatient, and demanding, but he'd never inflicted harm on her. Honesty also forced her to admit to herself that he hadn't been the one to destroy her world and deprive her of her identity. Others had, however. It was the others she constantly worried about, because they were part and parcel of Noah Sutton's high-powered lifestyle.

"Have I, Maggie?"

Some of her anger fled. "No," she whispered.

"Do you honestly think I would?"

She studied him, then conceded, "Not deliberately."

"Not *ever*," he corrected. "I'd walk away from you right now if I thought our relationship placed you in harm's way."

"Then why challenge me with puzzles when you could just as easily tell me straight out what your motives really are?"

"You need to rethink all of your reactions to people. You're defensive to the point of blinding yourself to the good side of life. If you don't get a firm handle on your reactions, your fate is sealed by your fear. Your life will be as empty as mine has been in recent years, although for different reasons. Is that what you want?"

His bluntness, not just honesty about himself, shocked her, shocked her enough that, without fully realizing what she was doing, she moved forward into his arms. He embraced her, a heavy sigh escaping him. For a fleeting moment she felt like a homing pigeon that had finally accomplished the last leg of a lengthy journey. The feeling jarred her, but it also offered unexpected comfort.

A war of uncertainty raged within her heart. She knew that the risks were monumental. It meant granting others power over her, something she'd vowed never to do again.

She remembered being Randall's pawn. State had stepped in after his death, orchestrating her life, then managing her right out of existence. The potential for abuse if she allowed anyone to victimize her with their power aroused every self-protective instinct she owned. Despite that awareness, Maggie succumbed to the undeniable sensation of safety she found in Noah's embrace. She'd begun to trust him, begun to hope that she might be able to have friendships and a normal life again, but at what price? she wondered. At what price?

Noah didn't press her after that. Maggie remained subdued and thoughtful as they inspected the grounds, the swimming pool, the tennis courts, and the two guest cottages situated on the opposite side of the sprawling garden.

They returned to her home in Monterey as plump banks of ground fog moved in from the Pacific. Not an uncommon event in the coastal communities during the late spring and early summer months, the diminished visibility forced Noah to concentrate on his driving and eliminated the need for conversation. Maggie appreciated the quiet.

"Would you be willing to take on the decorating detail?" Noah finally asked as he guided the car the final few miles to her home.

Maggie gave him a doubtful look. "For a place that size, you should probably hire a professional decorator."

He shook his head. "I want someone I trust in charge."

"It could take several months."

"You're too busy to do it?"

"I'm not busy at all, and you know it. That was my plan."

"You did mention you have the summer to yourself."

She nodded, pondering both the unresolved confrontation they'd had a short while ago and his request.

"You'd have carte blanche."

"Sounds like fun, but what if you hate it when I've finished?"

"That won't happen," he said with utter certainty.

She articulated a thought she'd had as they'd toured his future home. "How about a deep forest-green as the primary color for carpeting, with pale rose and crisp whites in tile and fabric for the furniture in order to soften the impact a little?"

"Bring the garden inside?"

Maggie nodded, pleased by his ability to conceptualize what she could already see in her own mind. "But without placing any emphasis on the florals. They can stay in the garden."

He smiled as he glanced at her when they paused at a stoplight. "You know me very well."

She laughed. "All I have to do is look at you."

She glanced pointedly at the deep green cotton sweater and crisp white trousers he wore. For as long as she'd known him, Noah had been what she thought of as a contrast dresser. He loved strong, warm colors blended with more temperate colors so that the balance complimented his darkly attractive features and athletic body. He possessed an innate sense of style, unusual for men in the diplomatic world who generally favored ultraconservative navy blue or charcoal-gray suits as their standard uniform. Gossip columnists across the globe had often commented on Noah's panache, and they hadn't just been referring to his taste in models.

"Will you do it?" he asked as he pulled up in front of her cottage and turned off the car engine.

She nodded. "I'll do it."

"You're a lifesaver." He exited the car and walked around to open the door for her.

"Actually, I'm probably crazy."

He slipped his arm around her shoulders and hugged her. "The right kind of crazy, as far as I'm concerned."

She made a fist and playfully tapped it against his midsection, her smile slipping somewhat as she encountered hard muscle. Her senses chose that moment to remind her of his rugged masculinity and the inescapable appeal of his toned body. It was a reminder Maggie knew she didn't really need. Noah tempted her enough.

He brought her hand to his lips and pressed a kiss to her knuckles, then led her up the walkway. "What's for dinner?" he asked as they paused at the front door.

Maggie burst out laughing. "You're hopeless."

He gave her a wounded look. "No, ma'am, I'm just hungry."

"Then I guess I'll have to feed you."

"I'm counting on it."

"You're being drafted as the cook's helper."

"I'm your devoted servant for the duration."

"Right," she said, her good humor restored by his teasing.

They worked side by side in the kitchen, lingering at the dinner table over the end result, which was a satisfying meal of cioppino, a spinach salad, and a fruity white wine from a nearby vineyard. Noah left shortly before midnight, a chaste kiss on Maggie's cheek marking his departure. She'd felt his desire for her, though, felt it in the faint tremor of his hands at her shoulders and in the subtle but very perceptible tightening of his anatomy when he'd briefly drawn her into his arms. She already knew that he wanted her, and she wondered if he felt as surprised as she did by the undercurrent of desire flowing back and forth between them.

As unsettling to her nerves and senses as Noah could be at times, Maggie reflected later as she got ready for bed, she delighted in his company. His agile mind and irreverent humor relaxed her. He charmed, he challenged, and he aroused her, the latter reaction seductive and thoroughly startling to a woman who had summarily closed herself off from feeling anything but wariness for other people.

She'd felt herself responding to him all evening. To the scent of his aftershave when he'd joined her in front of the stove and reached around her to help stir the simmering pot of fresh seafood. To the feel of his strong hands at her waist when he'd steadied her atop the footstool she always used to retrieve a particular serving bowl from an upper cupboard. To the brush of his fingertips when he'd passed the pepper shaker to her at the dinner table.

Although she'd counseled herself not to behave impulsively with him, she hadn't been able to ignore her heightened awareness of his innate sensuality. Her pulse raced each time he touched her. Her heart swelled when he voiced his admiration for the warmth of her home. And she no longer felt the customary fear that came with attention being directed at her.

What she experienced seemed . . . normal, even though her nerves felt tied in knots thanks to the sensations rushing recklessly through her, sensations that made her profoundly aware of her needs as a woman. Needs never truly satisfied.

Maggie acknowledged the fact that she'd never before thought of Noah in sensual terms. She did now, though. Constantly. Noah provoked the fragile fantasies of genuine trust in a relationship with a man, of being valued for herself as an individual, of the possibility of being loved—fantasies that she'd cast aside long ago. He inspired hope, as well, but the emotion was a double-edged sword, and it still frightened her. She didn't expect her fear to depart simply because she felt inclined to escort it to the front door. She had to confront the cause, and she needed to do it soon.

She silently cursed those who'd crippled her ability to feel and to embrace a normal life, because she now recognized the truth that Noah had spoken earlier in the day. She did need to rethink all of her reactions to people. If she didn't, she would remain an emotional cripple. The prospect of spending the rest of her life in that condition prompted her to also consider the possibilities of a relationship with Noah, perhaps even an intimate relationship at some point in the future.

Maggie finally drifted off to sleep, her final thought that she might not understand all of his motives yet, but that using her was not a part of the reason that Noah had come back into her life.

As she spent time with Noah in the days that followed, Maggie sensed that many of their individual needs were also mutual needs, even if the causes were quite different. Noah seemed genuinely lonely. He even spoke of the absence of emotional intimacy in his life. He'd apparently reached a pivotal crossroads, and, recognizing that, was trying to make changes that would allow him to be more content as a person. His honesty and courage inspired her. Maggie made a conscious decision to trust the fledgling instincts that were emerging within herself, instincts nurtured by Noah during their shared days and evenings.

Maggie also worked at coming to terms with the fear that had driven her to maintain a solitary lifestyle in recent years. Even though she felt justified in her past reactions, she now saw the wisdom of being guided in the future by positive emotions. Noah, by the sheer force of his determination to make a place for himself in her isolated world, had forced her to recognize the necessity of reevaluating her perspectives. She also found the strength to accept the fact that she'd surrendered control of her own destiny to those who had terrorized her, to those who had caused her to live in constant fear that what remained of her life would be torn from her once again.

Noah had implied as much during more than one of their conversations. She concluded through honest self-examination that he was right on target. His comments, although difficult to digest at times, helped her realize that she'd inadvertently done the one thing she'd tried not to do in the aftermath of Randall's duplicity and betrayal. She'd relinquished control of her life by constructing an invisible prison for herself and her emotions. In effect, she'd given her persecutors precisely what they'd wanted after they'd done everything in their power to cut her off from the world she'd known.

Maggie recommitted herself to a fresh start, the process enhanced by Noah's compassion and support as they began lining up contractors for painting, wallpapering, and tile and carpet installation at his new home. She blossomed, despite the demands of the schedule imposed by his proposed move-in date. Her smile appeared more readily, her wariness markedly decreased, and her confidence in herself grew. She began to feel like a new woman.

Other than the time he devoted to his professional concerns via computer and a fax machine in his hotel suite each morning, Noah spent virtually every waking hour at her side. Maggie savored the sense of partnership she experienced with him. She enjoyed watching him interact with the people they encountered, whether a furniture showroom salesman, a street mime, or the flamboyant owner of an eclectic art gallery on a Carmel side street.

She heard the depth of his commitment to his third world clients when he spoke of the poverty that plagued their nations. They discussed politics, but only in general terms. Maggie felt surprisingly unthreatened by the reminders of the past they shared, and she said as much to Noah. He'd kissed her soundly, then changed the subject. She felt like he'd given her a gold star.

They dined out as often as they ate in. They indulged their mutual passion for good films, debated daily the merits of the *San Francisco Examiner's* editorial page, and took long walks on the beach, regardless of the weather. She responded to Noah in ways that she'd thought lost to her. Laughter hallmarked their days, but they also shared lapses into silence with the same ease as lively conversation.

Maggie relaxed more and more. Her awareness of Noah as a virile man and potential lover began to dominate her senses and her thoughts, though, especially late at night when she felt too nerved up to sleep. She started to wonder if she'd misread his interest in her, because he never pushed beyond hand-holding when they strolled the beach, hugs at the conclusion of their days together, and hard little kisses that sizzled on her lips long after he'd driven back to his hotel.

She wanted him, she realized one afternoon as she stood at the top of the staircase in the main house of the estate as she waited alone for the delivery of furniture purchased the previous week. She wanted him with a depth of hunger that shook her to her core. She trusted him now. Completely. She was also—even though it stunned her to even think it—falling in love with him. It had taken her time to put the pieces together, but she finally had.

She loved Noah, loved him beyond the boundaries of friendship, loved him with the kind of unconditional acceptance that embraced the entire man, loved him in a way that she'd never loved Randall. It was the kind of love her grandmother had once told her was the purest. She felt that now. It unnerved her, but it also gave her an unexpected feeling of inner strength. She could feel again. Really feel.

Maggie slammed her open palm against the banister as she descended the staircase. "Damn! What in the world am I going to do now?"

"How about giving me a hug and telling me what's wrong?" Noah suggested as he walked out of the kitchen, crossed the foyer, and approached her.

She jumped at the sound of his voice. "Where did you come from?"

"The garage. Does it matter?"

Flustered by his unexpected appearance, Maggie brought her hands together in front of her. When Noah frowned at the gesture, a clear indication in the past of extreme stress on her part, she let her arms fall to her sides. *He knows me too well,* she thought in frustration.

"Does it matter, Maggie?" he asked a second time, pausing at the foot of the staircase and looking up at her.

Desire welled up inside her as she studied him, desire and a kind of soul-deep longing that made her want to walk straight into his arms and beg him to make love to her. *I'm in trouble. Deep and serious trouble.*

"Maggie?"

"It doesn't matter," she hastily assured him. She descended the stairs, intending to walk past him and into the kitchen. "I need to check on something."

He gently caught her arm. "Did I startle you?"

She nodded, but she couldn't bring herself to look up at him.

Noah slid his fingertips beneath her chin, forcing her to lift her face for his inspection. "Problem?"

"No."

"All right." Releasing her, he stepped out of her way.

Maggie immediately missed his touch. She also felt like the perfect fool as she backed away from him. Turning, she forced herself to walk slowly into the kitchen. She picked up speed once she got there, then made a beeline for the French doors that led out onto the terrace. Fresh air, she decided, would help her clear her head and regain her emotional balance before facing Noah again.

It was a good plan, but it failed.

Noah followed her.

"I think we need to talk," he said as he watched her pace the terrace.

She paused, exhaled raggedly, then said in a rush, "This isn't a good time. The furniture people are due any time now. Why don't we talk tomorrow? I have laundry to do tonight, and I need to pay some bills. It's almost the first of the month, you know." Shut up! she told herself.

Noah smiled. She wanted to smack the expression of amusement right off his face. That's when she knew she was becoming irrational, and she made an effort to regain control of herself.

He laughed. Outrage nearly swamped her, obliterating her efforts to calm herself.

"I can't help myself," he said in his own defense as he straightened out his mouth.

Her temper exploded. "If you think I'm so funny, then you can just laugh yourself right back into that house, mister. I'm leaving. You'll need the paperwork on the kitchen counter when the delivery people arrive. Have a nice afternoon."

Maggie charged down the flagstone steps.

Noah quietly asked, "Where's your purse?"

She stopped dead in her tracks. "In the kitchen," she muttered, making the return trip up the stairs and across the terrace. She kept her car keys in her purse, and they both knew it. Maggie flashed him a firm look. "I don't have anything to say, so don't you dare start grilling me."

Noah's expression sobered. He also followed her for the second time in as many minutes.

Maggie retrieved her purse from the kitchen cupboard and turned to find Noah standing squarely in front of her. He resembled a barricade. She choked down a sound of utter frustration, then glared at him.

He moved toward her, his expression no longer filled with humor. He looked every bit the implacable negotiator now, the man capable of playing hardball if the need arose.

"I have to leave," she said breathlessly.

His expression intent and his gaze piercingly

direct, he shook his head as he reached for her. "You need something else altogether."

She pressed back against the kitchen counter, the smooth granite edge digging into her lower back as she tried to evade him. A useless endeavor, she quickly realized as he captured her by the waist with one hand, relieved her of her purse with the other, and jerked her forward.

"What do you think you're—?"

"Be quiet, Maggie. Just be quiet."

"But—"

He smothered the sputtering sound she made, silencing her with his mouth. His beautiful, sensual mouth. She jerked beneath him, the shock of the intimate contact exploding across the landscape of her senses like a flamethrower. She moaned, her lips parting as she angled her head and welcomed his seductive assault.

This was different, she realized. This wasn't one of those hard little kisses she'd grown accustomed to. He was different. Noah fed on her like a man starved for the very essence of her, his hunger an unnecessary catalyst to the desire Maggie already felt. This was the man who'd almost made love to her on a darkened pier so many weeks ago. This was the man who'd been at her side as she'd opened her prison doors and stepped out into the sunlight. This was the man she'd begun to love and crave twenty-four hours a day.

She melted against him. She instantly felt the burn of his desire. It imprinted itself on her senses, saturated her flesh, and sank into her bones.

Maggie trembled violently, but she also gave as good as she got. She couldn't drink deeply enough of him, couldn't satisfy the frantic need she suddenly felt to touch him as her hands swept up his chest, her nails digging into his broad shoulders before she tangled her fingers at his nape.

Noah shuddered, his mouth consuming her, his hands anchoring her hips to his loins. She felt his arousal, felt the force of it and instinctively surged against him. She longed to absorb him into her flesh, longed to be absorbed.

He tore his mouth free, then drove his fingers into her thick hair as he framed her face between his palms. She stared up at him, desire glazing her wide blue eyes.

"I want you."

She knew that, but it still came as a shock to hear him say the words. "I—"

"Parker House Furniture!" a strange male voice shouted. "I've got a delivery for you folks."

Noah muttered a curse. Maggie pulled free of him, still shaken by the liquid fire flooding her bloodstream.

"Don't run from me this time, Maggie-mine."

She met his gaze. "Running's not an option. I can barely move."

"I'll deal with the delivery."

She nodded, struggling for poise. "I really do need to get home."

"Then what?"

Maggie sighed. "I'm not sure."

"It had to happen."

She summoned her courage. "I'm not sorry, Noah, but I'd like some time to think."

He brought his hand up again, and she didn't resist when he stroked her cheek with his fingertips. "Don't overanalyze, all right?"

She smiled ruefully. "You know me too well, Noah Sutton."

"Not nearly well enough. Not nearly well enough."

She heard regret, but she heard other emotions as well, even though she still felt too off balance to try and define them. She turned her head and pressed a kiss into the center of his palm, startling herself with the spontaneous gesture. When she met his gaze, Maggie realized that she'd startled Noah, as well.

"I'm not frightened," she whispered. "Just a little shaky."

He drew her close, holding her so tenderly that she had to bite her lip to keep herself from revealing the depth of her feelings for him.

"Hey, folks!" said a burly man in coveralls as he strode into the kitchen. "I'm on a tight schedule today."

Maggie rolled her eyes. "Good luck," she whispered to Noah before reclaiming her purse and slipping out the French doors.

SIX

Even though it was one of the toughest things he'd ever done, Noah left Maggie alone that evening. He forced himself not to call her or go after her, because he sensed that pushing her right now would be an error in judgment. He knew they needed to talk, but the foundation they'd built during the preceding weeks was still fragile and he didn't want to damage it.

Noah realized that he'd behaved impulsively, but he felt no guilt, in large part because Maggie hadn't reacted badly to the sensually charged scene at the estate. Her shock had been apparent, not simply her desire. They'd both been shaking from it when they'd been interrupted. He'd tasted the totality of her passion, felt the purity of her desire so deeply, so profoundly that she now seemed etched into his soul.

Her response had spawned hope within his

heart, but also caution and a renewed effort at the kind of patience that he rarely exercised in a relationship with a woman. He wanted her, wanted her with an intensity that still stunned him. When, he wondered, had he felt so compelled to possess a woman? The answer was simple. Never.

He spent a restless night, rising even earlier than usual the following morning when the hotel operator woke him with an urgent call from London. Noah dealt with the crisis that had occurred during an economic summit that was being handled by a trusted associate, then arranged a conference call with all the parties involved in order to assure himself that the participants were once again committed to setting aside grievances over long-standing border disputes and working for the common good of their nations.

Once he felt confident that the meetings were back on track, Noah tried to spend his escalating inner tension with a long run on the beach. He then showered and dressed for the day. His tension persisted, however, but he worked at concealing it as he drove to Maggie's shortly before noon.

She emerged from the side yard as he pulled up in front of her cottage. Her welcoming smile startled him, but he said a silent prayer of thanks and allowed himself to relax a little.

"Good morning."

He glanced at his watch. "It won't be in another five minutes or so."

"How are you?" she asked as she tucked her

gardening shears into the shallow basket she carried.

Filled with an array of long-stemmed roses from her garden, the contents of the basket reminded Noah of a fragrant rainbow. "Not too bad. How about you?"

"All right."

She climbed the stairs to the porch, her shapely legs drawing his attention. He remained at the bottom of the steps, the desire pummeling his senses so compelling, he couldn't get past it. The image of those legs encircling his hips held him in thrall, made a joke of his determination to control the hunger he felt for this woman. He wanted her. Wanted to experience every fantasy he'd ever had about her. Wanted to devastate her banked passions until she grew wild with the kind of need that only he could satisfy.

"Noah?"

"What?" he answered sharply, his voice equal parts ground glass and gravel.

She gave him a puzzled look. "Why don't you come inside? Lunch is ready."

Taken aback by her calm, Noah marshaled his wits and silently accepted her invitation. As they walked into the cottage, he glanced at the small dining table in the alcove adjacent to the kitchen, noting the two place settings, a platter of sandwiches and individual salads, and the pitcher of iced lemonade. Clearly, she'd expected him, and his predictability where Maggie was concerned didn't escape his notice.

"Looks good," he remarked.

She smiled a second time, but her expression seemed achingly vulnerable to Noah. He realized then that she felt the same sense of uncertainty that he'd been experiencing since the previous afternoon.

"Let's sit down," she suggested after placing the basket of roses on the counter in the kitchen.

"Yes, ma'am."

He helped her with her chair before taking his own. He also let Maggie set the pace of their conversation.

"Did all the library furniture we ordered from Sackett's make it onto the truck?" she asked as she reached for her napkin.

He nodded. "Every last piece."

"I forgot to tell you that the hardware for the drapery was supposed to be delivered yesterday, as well. If it didn't show up, I need to call Jack McGuire, since he's scheduled to stop by tomorrow and do the installation for you. He's also planning on coming back next week to do the shutters for the guest cottages."

"Everything arrived. The delivery schedule in your file was self-explanatory. You're still the most squared away female I've ever known."

She smiled. "You sound like a sexist drill instructor."

He scowled at her. "I've been told often enough that I have the personality of one."

"You're sure the reference wasn't to Attila the Hun?"

"Real nice, Ms. Holden."

"Be good," she teased, "or I'll send you and your sandwich out onto the porch."

"Yes, ma'am." He managed a sloppy salute and then devoted his attention to the food in front of him. The desire he felt for her didn't ease, though, and he resigned himself to being in a state of nearly painful arousal for the rest of his natural life. He grimaced at the thought, then bit into his sandwich like a man who hadn't eaten in weeks. His appetite for her didn't diminish at all. He suspected it never would.

"If things continue to go this smoothly, you'll be able to move in next week," Maggie remarked.

"The move-in date's etched in stone, as far as I'm concerned."

"You'll have a home soon, Noah."

He nodded abruptly. The look on her face, not just her softly spoken words, assured him that she finally understood how important it had become to him to turn that particular fantasy into a reality.

They chatted as they ate, touching briefly on a variety of neutral topics—the rain that had fallen during the night, the recent good fortune of Wall Street investors courtesy of an upturn in the stock market, and the petty behavior of the economic summit attendees that Noah had dealt with earlier that morning.

He helped Maggie clear the table once they finished their meal. Despite his best efforts to hold his concern at bay, her continued avoidance of the events that had taken place the previous afternoon started to gnaw on his nerves.

"I'm not going to bother with these now," she said once she rinsed the dishes and stacked them in the sink.

"Feel like taking a drive up to San Francisco this coming Saturday? I managed to get tickets for The Harlem Dance Studio."

Surprise shone in her expressive eyes, making them look like polished sapphires. "But that performance has been sold out for weeks! It's their only night in the city on their current tour."

Noah gently tapped the end of her nose. "Stick with me, kid. I've got an inside track."

"Obviously."

"Then we'll go."

"Thank you, Noah. I haven't been to the ballet in months. I've missed it."

"How about a walk on the beach this afternoon?" he asked.

"Maybe later," she answered as she led the way to the sunporch at the rear of the cottage.

Maggie paused in front of the wall of glass that provided a view of her rose garden. Noah stood behind her. Placing his hands on her shoulders, he tugged her backward. She settled against him without hesitation, her head falling back against his shoulder. A shaky sigh escaped her as he circled her waist with his arms, his fingers meeting as he pressed them against her midriff.

"We need to talk about yesterday."

"I know," she replied so softly that he had to strain to hear her words.

"Are you sorry it happened?"

She slowly turned to face him. "I'm not sorry at all. Why would I be?"

Relieved, he asked, "What are you, if you're not sorry?"

Maggie pondered his question for a long moment. "A little nervous. Fearful of destroying the friendship we've been working to rebuild. Concerned that I might be responding to you for the wrong reasons. Worried about being used again, even though I don't think you'd do it deliberately. Surprised that I can feel anything for anyone. Afraid to reach out for what I want, because it might be snatched away from me." She exhaled, the sound as tattered as the edges of an old flag. "All of the above, and a lot more, I guess. I haven't had time to think it all through yet."

"I have."

She gave him a bemused look. "Why doesn't that surprise me?"

"I've had a lot of years to think about things, Maggie-mine. More years than you can imagine."

She frowned. "I don't understand."

"I know, but I think you eventually will."

"What happens now?" she asked with the kind of directness that reminded him of the woman who'd once worked for him. Cut to the bottom line. Another shared characteristic.

"That's pretty much up to you."

"I don't want to be rushed."

He understood her caution, and he respected it in spite of the desire raging through his body even now. "I won't rush you," he promised.

"This might be a simple case of chemistry running amok."

He chuckled, the sound rustling like fallen leaves. "Perhaps, but I don't think so. We're both old enough to know the difference between chemistry and emotion."

"Maybe we're both just lonely," she speculated, her tone of voice troubled.

"We're both a lot of things, Maggie. Being lonely's only one part of a very complicated equation."

"Whatever's going on, I'd like to find out what it all means, but carefully, please."

"Very carefully," he vowed as he tenderly drew her against him and held her.

Maggie slipped her arms around his waist and pressed her cheek against the hard wall of his chest. Noah once again put the brakes on the need that scorched his insides and hardened his anatomy. He'd just made her a promise that he intended to keep, even if he died from the strain of not expressing his hunger for her. His encircling arms tightened. He exhaled so raggedly that he drew Maggie's curious gaze.

"What?" she asked.

"I guess it's my turn to be surprised."

"Why?"

"I expected you to head for the nearest exit."

Maggie reached up and smoothed a fingertip across his lower lip, then pressed her hand against the side of his angular face. "There's no place left to hide, and it's time for me to take a stand. You've been very patient with me, but you were right when you said I needed to rethink my responses. I'm also not afraid of your puzzle any longer. Given time, I'll solve it." She paused, studying him for a long moment then said, "Before anything happens between us, though, we'll have to talk about Randall, and I'm just about ready to have that conversation."

"Maggie . . ."

"It's necessary, Noah. More necessary than you can possibly imagine."

"I don't agree," he said.

"You don't have to agree, but I expect you to listen to what I have to say."

He looked at her, his eyes reflecting his doubt about the wisdom of a conversation about a dead man whom he despised, and then he nodded reluctantly. "Fair enough."

"It is fair, and I will always need that kind of consideration from you. I've finally figured out that I have a right to expect it in all my relationships."

Noah understood then that she'd rediscovered her courage and her confidence. He wanted to believe that he'd contributed to the process in some way, but he knew in his heart that he'd been little more than a momentary catalyst.

Maggie deserved to take all the credit for confronting her ghosts and making the decision to reverse the course of a life that, until now, had been orchestrated by others. He realized that he'd never loved or respected her more than he did at that moment. He also felt optimistic that she would soon be willing to reclaim more than just selected portions of her life.

A few days later Maggie stood in the kitchen at the estate. She set aside the scissors and the last roll of shelf paper. Scanning the interior of the cupboards, she felt satisfied with the result of her efforts. "That's finally done."

"What's finally done?" Noah asked as he walked into the estate's kitchen. He placed the hammer and screwdriver he'd been using to assemble a computer table on the counter.

"The kitchen and pantry shelves."

"You've been at it for hours."

"Just being thorough," she said with a smile as she gathered up stray clippings from the countertop and deposited them in a nearby trash can.

"Besides, this isn't exactly a small kitchen. It's nearly restaurant-sized."

He glanced into an open cupboard. "You always are. Thorough, I mean."

She smiled. "Just say thank you, Noah."

He seized her by the waist and brought her into his heat. "How about a hug, instead?"

She laughed, loving the feel of his muscular body and the relaxed pleasure she heard in his voice. Lifting her arms, she wrapped them around his neck. She felt encompassed but not overwhelmed by his embrace, and she savored the feeling.

"Guess I'd better buy some pots and pans. Maybe even some dishes."

Startled by his remark, she leaned back in his arms and peered up at him. "What have you been using all these years? Paper plates?"

He nodded, looking almost boyish as he confessed, "I usually eat out."

"You're hopeless."

"But eminently trainable," he assured her.

She grinned. "I expect you are."

He nuzzled the side of her neck, his lips and the tip of his tongue leaving a tingling trail of heat. "I'm glad you think so, Maggie-mine."

Her grin faded as desire spiraled through her. "Kiss me," she whispered as she turned her head and went in search of his lips. She found them, leisurely stroking his lower lip with the tip of her tongue, then nibbling on it with gentle teeth.

Noah lifted her, eased her into a seated position on the kitchen counter, and moved between her parted thighs, all without breaking contact. He gripped her waist and intensified their connection, his tongue thrusting deeply.

As their lips fused, Maggie smoothed her palms across his broad shoulders, her fingers eventually digging into the muscular expanse. She tasted the scorching intensity of his desire, and it reminded her of a high-powered tension line. Stunning currents of pleasure invaded her body and stimulated her senses. Maggie moaned beneath the dip and glide of Noah's tongue as he explored her.

Noah inhaled the sound, his fingers measuring her narrow waist, then skimming steadily upward. He covered her breasts with his hands, fondling her through the T-shirt and bra she wore while simultaneously deepening their kiss.

She arched into his intimate touch, then trembled as she felt her breasts swell and her nipples tighten into aching points of sensation. The arousal she felt was acute, almost painful. Desire plunged into her veins like an invasion force assaulting a beachhead, and her heart soared with emotion. She felt nearly overwhelmed with hunger for him.

She longed to shed her clothing and embrace Noah within the confines of her body. Whatever anxiety she might have once felt at the prospect of moving beyond friendship, those feelings were gone, she realized. Trust and love had completely eclipsed them. She worried, though, that she might disappoint him with her lack of experience. Noah suddenly lifted his head, separating their mouths as he struggled for control. He shifted his hands to her waist, his grip almost fierce.

Thoroughly shaken by their exchange, Maggie buried her face against his neck and held on to him. His respiration sounded as uneven as her own, and she realized that they'd reached a point of no return. There were truths she needed to share. Once she had, she hoped he would still want her.

"Let's sit in the garden," he suggested, his voice still rough with barely contained desire.

Maggie nodded, grateful that he understood her need for the comfort she derived from that particular environment.

He stepped back, his expression strained. "Go ahead. I'll join you in a few minutes."

Maggie slipped off the counter, her knees almost buckling from the desire still swirling wildly within her. Noah steadied her.

"I want you so much," she said, certain that he must see the love shining in her eyes each time she looked at him.

"And I want you, Maggie-mine, but you said we needed to talk first."

She nodded. "Thank you for understanding."

She walked outside, grateful for a few minutes

of privacy to compose herself. An early-evening breeze calmed her as she sat on the stone bench in the center of the garden and collected her thoughts.

Noah joined her. Seated side by side in the fading sunlight, they shared the snifter of cognac he'd brought with him from the bar in the house.

"You never liked him, did you?" she asked, referring to her late husband.

"I loathed him."

"I never knew. You hid it well."

"I had no choice. We were friends, and you made it clear that he was the man you wanted."

"A lapse in judgment on my part, that's for sure."

"Don't put yourself down," Noah said.

"It's the truth. In the long run, it's better to simply deal with it and then move forward."

He nodded.

"I was twenty-four when I met Randall," she began, her voice far stronger than she actually felt. "I know you remember those days. We'd been working together for nearly three years by then, and, thanks to you, I'd already seen most of the world. He was ten years older than me, charming, intelligent, articulate, and on the fast track at State. Although I'd dated a few people before Randall, I hadn't ever been with a man."

"I always suspected as much," Noah remarked as he handed her the snifter.

She took a sip of cognac and returned the glass to him. "I fell in love with him very quickly, and he claimed to love me. He asked me to marry him almost immediately, but I insisted on a six-month engagement. I didn't want to rush into a lifelong commitment, despite my feelings for him. He hated the delay, but he tolerated it. I remember him saying that once we were married, he'd make the important decisions for us, because I had the instincts of a snail. At the time, I just thought he was expressing his sexual frustration. I didn't realize then that he was giving me an important clue about himself as a man."

"Randall was always in a hurry, Maggie. It caused his downfall."

She nodded. "I eventually discovered that grim little fact. He told me on our first wedding anniversary that he planned to be an ambassador before he turned forty. I quickly realized that he hadn't simply created a lofty goal for himself. He was obsessed with making that goal a reality. Our life together—every person we invited into our home, every embassy party we attended, every single word that came out of his mouth—was dedicated to making it happen. My background as a translator also figured into the equation. Randall called me his asset. I grew to hate that word after a while."

"He used you."

"Yes, he used me. My language skills, he once told me, were critical to his success. Anyway, if someone in his section at State received an embassy posting he thought should have been given to him, he would become uncontrollably angry. If another person's evaluation of a political hot spot received more praise by a department head, he'd spend hours maligning the man's abilities."

She glanced at Noah, whose expression was unreadable. "I was shocked by his bitterness and resentment. I'd never been around anyone who could hate the way Randall hated. It frightened me, because I knew he couldn't keep that side of himself a secret forever. He was ambitious, but self-destructively so. It was hard to watch, even harder to live with, but I'd taken vows that meant the world to me, so I redoubled my efforts to make him feel secure at home. I thought that if I could make him happy, he'd be less obsessed with his goals. I was wrong. The harder I tried to express my love for him and my confidence in him, the worse things became."

She brought her hands together in her lap. "I was relieved when we left Washington. It seemed like the perfect opportunity for a fresh start. I hoped that we could start a family, and I even thought Randall would regain his perspective about his professional agenda. It didn't happen. The years in Paris and Rome were a nightmare. The people who worked for him at the embassies hated him, even though they were always kind to me."

"Liking you's easy, Maggie."

"Randall resented it when people were nice to me. I paid a high price for their kindness, even though they never realized it."

"What kind of price?" Noah asked, his voice gratingly low.

She studied the brandy snifter, unable and unwilling to meet Noah's gaze. The shame she felt was on the verge of strangling her, but she knew she owed him the entire truth. "He was drinking heavily by then. When he drank, he was mean."

Noah swore, the sound vicious. "Did he hit you?"

She nodded, a painful memory rising up inside her and nearly preventing her from continuing, but she made herself go on. "I was pregnant, in my first trimester, when it happened. I miscarried from the fall I took. He seemed to get control of himself, at least for a while after that incident."

"Why in hell did you stay?" Noah demanded.

"Pride. Confusion. Fear. My parents were dead. I didn't know where to turn, and I was desperately ashamed. He convinced me at first that it was my fault that he'd hit me. He said I'd driven him to it. Then he begged me to give him another chance. Foolishly, I did. I didn't want my marriage to fail, so I learned to accommodate, learned never to challenge anything he said when he was drinking. Looking back, I know that the real abuse was emotional. It was like a form of terrorism, but it was so subtle at first, and then so sustained, that I didn't understand what was happening. I was too busy trying to stay one step ahead of his disapproval that, when I did finally see the situation for what it was, things had gotten completely out of control. He'd apparently become involved in some back alley liaison with people from a former eastern bloc country, although I didn't have a clue about his activities. I learned later that he was receiving money in exchange for government documents that he took from the ambassador's safe. My personal life was caving in around me, so I wasn't exactly up to speed on his machinations at the embassy. Randall made me doubt myself, made me question my judgments about everything with his driving need to control everyone around him."

"Why didn't you come to me?"

She glanced at him. "I couldn't. I wasn't your responsibility."

"But I would have helped you."

She shook her head. "You don't understand. I wasn't ready to help myself, and that's what it takes, Noah. A person in an abusive relationship has to save herself. It doesn't work if someone else tries to do it for you. My loyalty to Randall was totally misplaced, but it took me years to realize that I was honoring vows that didn't mean anything to him. After four or five years of his rules and his constant belittling, I didn't know if I was coming or going."

"What do you mean by rules?"

"There were rules for everything," she said, the weight of emotional fatigue in her voice as she spoke. "The people I was supposed to socialize with, the kind of meals I served to dinner guests, gifts for coworkers, sex, the condition of our home. You name it, there were rules for it. I honestly don't know why the security people at State thought I was involved in his documents-for-money game. They apparently monitored his every move that last year, so they should have realized that I was a virtual prisoner in my own home. I was on the verge of a breakdown when Randall was murdered and State hustled me out of Europe without so much as a change of clothes."

"Rules for sex?" Noah said quietly.

Maggie heard his shock. She didn't try to dodge it. "Despite how enlightened my parents were about almost everything, I didn't receive much guidance about intimacy from them when I was growing up. By the time I needed advice, my mother was dead." She exhaled softly. "I didn't like sex with him. Randall wasn't a thoughtful lover, and when I didn't respond to him, he became verbally abusive. I didn't have much confidence in that department to start with. My marriage undermined my confidence even more, and now I'm terrified that I'll disappoint you."

Noah set aside the brandy snifter and took her hands. "Look at me, Maggie."

She slowly shifted her gaze from their joined hands to his face.

"You're the most sensual woman I've ever held in my arms. I want you so much, my entire body aches twenty-four hours a day. I've wanted you for a long time. Randall Hartley was a duplicitous bastard. I'm not."

"What if you're wrong?" she whispered, wanting to believe him. "What if I'm incapable of pleasing you?"

"Trust me, I'm not wrong."

She just looked at him. She said a silent prayer that Noah was right, that what they'd shared during the last several weeks was a strong enough foundation for the kind of lovemaking she'd dreamed of experiencing with a man.

"You please me so much, it hurts to breathe when I hold you. Please trust me on that, all right?"

"I do trust you. You're the only man I've ever trusted, even though I was afraid to admit it to myself until recently."

"Forget Randall Hartley. He's dead and buried. If you let him haunt you, you'll be giving him the same power he once had over you."

She smiled faintly. "I've figured that out. Finally. I just felt that I should be totally honest with you about my past."

"It doesn't change anything. I still want you. I think I always will."

She sagged against him when he drew her into his arms.

"You're exhausted," he muttered as he held her.

"True, but I still want . . ."

He pressed a kiss to the top of her head. "We both want the same thing, but I care too much about you to rush you. As tough as it is to admit it to myself, you need more than a night in bed with me right now."

Maggie lifted her head and peered up at him. "I . . . I didn't think I'd ever be able to feel anything for a man again. I didn't think I'd ever want anyone to touch me that way. It's different with you, though. I feel so much. It's rather unsettling at times."

He cupped her face between his hands. "Once we make love, I won't be able to let you walk away, so you need to be certain it's really what you want."

She stared at him, startled by his words and his intensity. "All right, but if you change your mind, I'll understand."

"I won't change my mind."

Maggie believed him. She smiled, realizing that the final burden from her past had finally been consigned to the refuse heap. She felt freer than she'd felt in years.

He stood, then drew her to her feet. Slipping his arms around her, he held her for several lingering minutes. Maggie felt his desire for her in the tightening of his body, but she also felt Noah's self-imposed restraint.

Was this kind of consideration normal in a relationship between a man and a woman? she wondered. Was this how a man behaved when he loved a woman?

She pressed a kiss to his chin. "Thank you."

"For what?"

"For being you. You're an unexpected gift."

He looked embarrassed and doubtful. "If you say so."

"I say so."

SEVEN

Two evenings later Maggie cast another amazed glance at the itemized household goods list she held. "For a man who's spent most of his adult life living out of suitcases and in hotels, you certainly have a lot of stuff." She checked off yet another numbered carton. "Two hundred and fourteen cartons of books at last count. Noah, you could open your own library."

He smiled at her as he popped the lid on another carton. "So shoot me. I happen to like browsing through bookstores when I travel."

Almost obscured from view by seven-box-high towers created by the movers, she grinned back at him from across the room. "I hate to be the one to break it to you, but this is an obsession, not an example of browsing."

"Good thing we have lots of bookcases, isn't it?"

"You can say that again."

"Good thing . . ."

She groaned.

He pointed his finger at her, pretending that it was a pistol.

Laughing, Maggie sank into the nearest chair. "I think I need a break."

"It's been a long couple of days," he conceded as he set aside the single-edge blade he'd been using to open the cartons, dusted his hands on the thighs of his jeans, and crossed the room.

The expression on his face prompted Maggie to ask, "You're happy, aren't you?"

He nodded as he paused in front of her and tugged her to her feet. Turning her so that she faced away from him, Noah brought his hands to her shoulders and began to work the knots from her tight muscles. "Very happy, Maggie-mine."

She moaned, her head falling forward. "You've got a thousand years to stop that."

"Feel good?"

She felt his fingers penetrate the ache in her shoulders while his thumbs circled rhythmically at the base of her neck. Other sensations followed, sensations that made her knees weak and her breathing choppy. "Good's too tame a word. I think I died and went to heaven."

He pressed a kiss to the side of her neck as he continued. She unraveled inside like a spinning top, his touch simultaneously relaxing her muscles and arousing her senses. Her heart trembled, her emotions quickly rising to the surface.

"Are you ready for a glass of wine?"

Although they'd scattered somewhat, she found her wits and answered him. "Sounds tempting. Any idea of the time?"

"It's late. Probably near midnight."

"I need to get home. We have another long day ahead of us tomorrow."

He lifted his hands from her shoulders and slid his arm around her waist. "Rest and relaxation first. We both need to unwind a little."

Forcing aside the desire she felt, Maggie smiled up at him as they walked out of the library. Instead of leading her to the downstairs kitchen, Noah guided her across the second-floor landing and into another wing of the house.

Maggie remarked, "I think you missed a left turn."

"Trust me."

She did, she realized as she gazed up at his profile. She trusted him as much as she loved him—completely—although she knew he didn't have any idea of the depth of her feelings for him yet. They were still too new, too tender to expose. And a part of her still feared that she might make a fool of herself if she revealed them.

During the previous few days she'd been satisfied to drift with her emotions, to accustom herself to the idea of welcoming Noah into her heart and her bed. She knew he wanted her. How could she not know, even though he put no pressure whatsoever on her? He seemed committed to giving her the space she needed to come to terms with their relationship. His compassion and the absence of pressure since their conversation about Randall still amazed her, but she now considered it a mixed blessing.

She appreciated his patience, but only up to a point. She wanted him. Wanted him so much that she couldn't sleep through the night any longer, couldn't think about anything or anyone but him when they were apart, and couldn't figure out a way of bringing that little fact to his attention without throwing herself at him. She'd managed not to so far, but she seriously doubted that she would be able to restrain herself much longer.

Maggie still marveled over his sudden reappearance in her life. As recently as six weeks ago, she'd been getting from one day to another, her life the equivalent of an endurance test. Now, though, she embraced each new dawn with a sense of anticipation that possessed the power to amaze her. Noah, by stubbornly encouraging her to come out of hiding and by sharing simple pleasures with her, had helped her find the strength to begin living and feeling again.

They walked into the master suite. Maggie loved this part of the house. Spacious and luxurious, it felt like a retreat. The vibrant deep green carpet and the crisp white walls and linens simultaneously contrasted and soothed.

"What do you think of our handiwork?" Noah asked as he released her and strode to the bar in the adjacent sitting room.

Her gaze snagged on the king-size bed that dominated the master bedroom, and she had to force herself past the image that suddenly popped into her head of the two of them in it. "It's my favorite part of the house. The library runs a close second, though, in spite of all those blasted book cartons still stacked to the ceiling."

"Make yourself comfortable."

She followed him into the sitting room and sat down on one of the love seats. Watching him as he removed the cork from a bottle of white wine, she eased her feet out of her deck shoes and tucked them beneath her. Noah joined her a few moments later, carrying a tray that held two filled wineglasses, a bowl of fresh strawberries, a dish of crackers and a wedge of Brie, and a stack of napkins.

She grinned, helping herself to a glass of wine and a napkin. "Good idea. You get an A plus."

"I thought you'd approve."

"I do," she said as she reached for a strawberry and dipped the tip of it into her wine before slipping the fruit into her mouth. Once she swallowed the morsel, she announced, "Perfect. I like the way your mind works."

"Glad to be of service," he teased as he joined her on the love seat.

She raised her wineglass, acknowledging his

thoughtfulness with a silent toast. As they relaxed and enjoyed their wine, Maggie became increasingly aware of Noah's nearness. The clock on an upper shelf of the entertainment center across the room pushed beyond the midnight hour.

The lingering scent of his aftershave taunted her. Nothing new about that, she reminded herself as she tried to contain her response to him. The flex and flow of his muscular thighs repeatedly drew her gaze. Nothing new about that, either, she thought as she forced herself to look at the painting that hung on a nearby wall.

She inhaled shakily, telling herself that this was neither the time nor the place to reveal her desire for him, but the instructions she directed at her libido fell on deaf ears when Noah casually claimed her free hand and pressed a kiss into the center of her palm after drinking the last of his wine and setting aside his glass. Maggie felt the impact of his sensuality right down to the soles of her bare feet.

Heated need surged to life inside her, scorching her bloodstream and accelerating her pulse into a hard gallop. She took a sip of her wine, but her fingers trembled and the wine sloshed, so she placed her glass on the coffee table before she dropped it.

Noah smeared the last of the Brie onto two crackers and handed her one. Maggie noticed yet again the way in which her fingers shook as she accepted his offering. This time, so did Noah.

He frowned. "You okay?"

She jerked a nod in his direction and popped the cheese-slathered cracker into her mouth.

He set aside his napkin. "You don't look okay. You're very pale."

She finished chewing and swallowed. "Just tired, I guess," she said without meeting his gaze. Desire streamed through her, stunning her with the force of emotion that accompanied it.

"Come here," he said as he took her hands.

She mutely shook her head, freed herself from his grasp, and got to her feet. Crossing the room, Maggie walked out onto the upper balcony and made her way to the railing. She gripped it tightly, the heat flooding her body like a fast-moving fireball.

Noah followed her. "What just happened?"

"Nothing," she answered, her voice hoarse, whispery.

"You're not making any sense," he told her. "If you don't feel well, just say so."

Maggie reacted defensively. "Don't, Noah. I'm not up to sparring with you tonight."

"Then give me another option. Talk to me."

The command in his voice set her teeth on edge and aroused feelings of vulnerability. "You sound very dictatorial right now."

"So sue me, but tell me what the hell's wrong."

"Nothing's wrong!" she cried, her control snapping once and for all. Maggie felt insane all of a sudden. Utterly insane. A voice in her head urged, Just tell the man you want him. Quit making things so complicated. "Oh, God, everything's wrong," she said, reversing herself without warning.

"Why?"

"I feel so inept right now."

"Are you ill?"

"Only if you classify yourself as a disease," she snapped before she pressed her hand to her mouth in horror.

He stared at her, then laughed, the sound coming from deep inside his body. Her nerve endings fluttered, her senses so fine-tuned to him now that she even responded to the sound of his laughter. It aroused. It infuriated. It also tortured.

Why haven't you made love to me? she almost shouted. *What are you waiting for? The next total eclipse?*

"I have to get home." She turned, but she didn't even manage to take the first step away from him before he reached out for her. She tried to evade him, but she failed.

He locked on to her wrists with both hands, his gaze steady as he looked at her. "You're finally ready for us, aren't you?"

Stunned by the rawness of his voice, not just his blunt question, she stared up at him, the light of the moon like a high wattage streetlamp that revealed the strain she felt. "I don't . . ." Liar, her conscience shouted, so she closed her mouth.

He tugged her forward a step. "Of course you do, Maggie-mine."

"Damn you," she said, but the words sounded like a caress as she spoke them. Something fragile inside of her tore free of its moorings. Her heart? she wondered.

"I'll only be damned if I can't make love to you."

A single tear slid down her cheek. She jerked a hand from his grasp and angrily brushed it away. "Sometimes I . . . I can't believe you're real."

"Or that I want you?"

Shaken by the compassion she heard in his deep voice, she nodded, beyond words now.

"I do, more than you can imagine."

She no longer had a choice, she realized, although she barely even heard his remark. The bond between them was too strong, the need within her too overpowering to be suppressed any longer. Maggie walked straight into his arms a heartbeat later, a ragged sigh of relief escaping her as she did precisely what she'd dreamed of doing for days now.

She stopped hiding from the desire she felt, stopped running from the need rooted in her heart and soul, stopped fighting the inevitable. She surrendered totally.

She trembled as he drew her into the heated tension of his body. Craving his passion, seeking his strength, and so hungry for his love that it still frightened her, Maggie slid her arms around his waist and lifted her face to him. "I need you."

He brought his hands up to frame her face, his fingers penetrating the thickness of her shoulder-length hair. He searched her features, as if to verify the truth of her admission. "You're sure?"

"Please, Noah."

He muttered a harsh word. "Don't beg, Maggie. I don't expect that of you. I never will."

Emotion rippled through her, emotion so powerful that she finally understood that she'd never truly loved before. She managed to nod, and she realized then that even if Noah never loved her, even if they weren't destined for a permanent commitment, she needed him, needed his honor and his passion. She secretly suspected that she would need those things from him for the rest of her life. For the present, however, she consciously decided to accept the reality of what they could share. Here and now.

Noah couldn't ignore the array of revealing emotions—apprehension, desire, and relief, to name a few—that he saw in Maggie's expressive eyes. He responded to them and to her, his hands reassuring as he held and stroked her trembling body.

Once she started to relax, he lifted her into his arms and cradled her against his chest. He carried her inside, pausing briefly to dim the lights in the master suite before walking to the bed and carefully lowering her onto it.

He knew he needed some distance from her, if only for a few moments. Desire streaked through his body like fire-tinged lava rushing pell-mell over the side of a cliff. He wanted her with an almost violent brand of need that shook him to his very core, and he feared overwhelming her with the consuming force of his hunger.

Noah drew back from her, but he paused as he felt the unexpected strength of her grip when she clutched at his hands. The worry in Maggie's eyes tore at him. "It's all right. I'm not going anywhere."

"Promise?"

"Promise. I couldn't leave you now if my life depended on it."

She looked startled. Noah smiled, his expression strained as he tried but failed to control the tension tremoring through the muscles of his body and delivering additional surges of heat to his loins. He burned for her, burned deep inside in parts of himself until now kept separate from any feelings he'd ever had for a woman.

With Maggie, however, restraint didn't exist and boundary lines disappeared. His heart was unguarded territory, his emotions more accessible and vulnerable than at any other time in his life. She was the mate he sought, and he would settle for no one else, but for now he still felt compelled to withhold the real truth of his feelings for her.

He sensed that she wouldn't believe pledges of love or vows of commitment. He doubted that her experiences with Randall would permit her to trust them quite yet. For now, he silently reminded himself, he would simply demonstrate his love.

His intent gaze prompted her to whisper his name.

He responded to her confusion. "I want you too much."

Her gaze traveled over his face, down his chest, then dipped lower. "I can see that," she breathed, looking up at him again.

He muttered a rough word, but it sounded very much like a fervent prayer as it passed his lips. He sank down beside her, drawing her into his arms. She burrowed against him, shoving his pulse into overdrive with the subtle but erotic undulations of her body as she fitted herself to him.

"I want you, too, Noah. So much so that I hurt inside."

Her honesty made his senses riot. He claimed her mouth then, the taste of her like a drug he'd craved but had been denied for far too long. He thrust his tongue deeply into her honeyed recesses, his caution abruptly abandoned as she angled her head and parted her lips even more.

Maggie moaned into his mouth, the sound so seductive that his arms tightened around her and fire lanced like shards of summer lightning into his groin. She hesitated just moments later, though, in such a way and so briefly that he almost missed it. He realized then that she'd suddenly become tentative, as if anticipating his rejection if she became overly aggressive. He felt a vague sense of disquiet as he drew back and looked down at her.

Sprawled on her back, her dense hair in disarray, her eyes half closed, and her lips still wet from his kiss, Maggie personified feminine invitation and stunning vulnerability.

"What are you thinking?" Noah asked, his hands framing her face as he recalled the rules she'd spoken of a few days earlier.

She glanced away.

"Tell me."

She finally met his gaze. The trepidation in her eyes made his insides clench with compassion.

"I feel so much when I'm with you, but I'm almost afraid to let it out. I know it's stupid."

"Don't ever hold back with me. I need everything you have to give. I'm starved for all of it," he admitted.

"You won't turn away from me, will you?"

He saw and heard her amazement. "I couldn't, even if I wanted to. I need you too much."

"Why me, Noah? I don't understand. You've had so many women."

He spoke with the simplicity and sincerity of a man who'd known genuine loneliness for many years. "They weren't you." He touched her cheek, his fingers shaking as he stroked her silky skin.

"Forget the past, Maggie-mine. Together we'll make new memories, the kind that won't destroy your confidence or make me feel empty inside. I want everything you have to offer."

She turned her head so that his fingertips grazed her lips. Her breath bathed them with moist heat, the sensuality of the gesture more instinct than design, Noah realized. In response, he brought the hand she'd placed against his chest to his mouth and pressed a kiss to her fingertips. Sucking a single digit into his mouth, he swirled his tongue around it. He continued until he'd kissed the fingertips of both her hands.

She stirred restlessly in his arms, her plump breasts pushing against his chest as she arched into him, her slim legs twining with his more powerful ones. She simmered with responsiveness and sensuality, so much so that the muscles in his large body felt stretched as tightly as newly strung piano wire. It infuriated him that anyone had ever placed restrictions on her innocently seductive nature, but another part of him, the selfish part, was glad that he would be the man to awaken and experience her true passion. Her inner fire was a part of her that he treasured, would always treasure if given the opportunity.

Maggie sighed as she shifted against him yet again. When she looked up at him, he saw the hope shining in her eyes that he really meant what he'd just said a few moments earlier.

"No rules, Maggie. Not ever. I swear it on everything I hold dear."

"I believe you." She curled into him, her mouth hungrily fastening to his, her hands sliding up his broad chest before they circled his neck.

He felt the last barriers of her restraint topple in the minutes that followed, but he took his time with her, lingering at her lips, delving past even white teeth to explore the heated flavors beyond, sipping, then drinking deeply of her, and then sipping again. She followed where he led, her tongue tangling with his, then darting into his mouth when he withdrew to tantalize with lazy sweeps and erotic little stabs that left a trail of sizzling firebursts across the landscape of his senses.

Her fingertips traveled over his chest, tactilely mapping the hard walls and the expanse of hair that covered it, flexing delicately when she moved on to measure the width of his shoulders, then pressing rhythmically against the back of his neck. He traced the contours of her body with his hands, his touch provocative, his desire for her endless, his craving to possess every curve and hollow of her driving him. He touched her and he tasted her, again and again, totally focused on her needs and his desire to saturate his own senses with her essence, then drown in the elemental fire that he knew burned with intensity deep in her soul.

He stroked her from shoulder to thighs, but he quickly became frustrated by the barrier of her clothing. Tugging the hem of her T-shirt free of her jeans, he pushed the material aside. He spanned her waist, his fingertips meeting at the base of her spine, smoothing upward over exposed skin, then moving forward to the front of her body. When Maggie squirmed to free herself from the fabric confining her, he took his cue from her, briefly separating their mouths as he drew the T-shirt over her head and tossed it aside.

Her hands frantic, Maggie found the buttons of his shirt a heartbeat later. Her lips followed, lingering over each expanse of flesh revealed below his throat. She trailed a path of openmouthed kisses across his collarbone, then began an erotic journey down his chest. She paused when Noah hastened the process, jerked his shirt free of his body, and dropped it onto the floor beside the bed.

He shuddered as she sank her fingers into the hair that covered his hard chest, kneading like a jungle feline in the throes of some sensory interlude, her nails raking over him but causing no pain. He shuddered even more violently a second time when she fingered his nipples, the flat discs hardening beneath her touch. She dipped her head, her tongue flicking over the sensitive terrain she'd just discovered. She sighed tremulously, her hot breath washing across his flesh.

Unable to restrain himself any longer, Noah shifted her onto her back and moved over her, smoothing his large hands over her breasts until she arched like a drawn bow, then flicking open the clasp of her bra with his fingertips. He brushed aside the flimsy material. She spilled free, firm creamy flesh tipped by taut, deep mauve buds that seemed to beg for his touch.

She sucked in a startled breath when he covered her with his hands, and he savored the softness of her skin and the contrasting tautness of her nipples. His mouth was voracious as he kissed her, his tongue tracing the slick contours of her lips, then dipping deeply inside to tantalize.

Maggie trembled. Her nipples tightened even more, stabbing into the centers of his palms. When Noah's hands clenched, his fingers molding her, shaping her, she groaned her pleasure.

She teethed his lower lip, taunting him, pushing him with the seductive gesture. He felt the escalating tensions that swirled through her like a gusting summer wind, felt it in the tremors that shook her body, felt it in the clasp of her fingers as she dug them into his muscular back. She grew breathless, and the little gasping sounds that escaped her riddled his nerve endings and heightened his desire for her even more.

Relinquishing her mouth, he moved down her body despite her inarticulate cries of displeasure. He crouched over her, his hands at the waistband of her jeans. Noah waited, though, waited for the dazed look in her eyes to clear, waited for her to comprehend his intent, despite the desire jetting hotly through his body. She did, approving it an instant later with a single nod.

She lifted her hips, helping him as he freed her of her remaining clothing, then watched him stand and shed his own. He felt the hot sweep of her gaze as it traveled over his already aroused body. He saw the subtle but definitive tremors that passed through her. The incinerating heat that seemed to emanate from her sent yet another rush of desire tunneling through his veins. The muscles of his body tightened even more, and he had to work to suppress the volatile impulses that threatened to overrun his control.

Maggie opened her arms to him, the gesture more eloquent and welcoming than any words she might have spoken at that moment. Noah joined her on the bed, drawing her close. He savored her eager embrace, not just the lushness of her body and the nearly scalding heat of her skin. He wanted to sink into her now, wanted to end years of torment, but he contained those impulses.

Maggie sensed Noah's restraint, but she no longer wanted it. Her need was too great, the result of almost primitive rhythms of desire battering her senses. She felt his arousal pressing against her abdomen. Her hands drifted down his body, and she intimately stroked him. He jerked under her evocative touch, his low groan flooding her mouth as he kissed her. She willingly drank in the sound, deriving satisfaction from the knowledge that he wanted her so much.

"Don't wait," she breathed against his mouth. "I need you inside me."

His flesh surged violently. He shuddered, but he didn't take her. Instead, he moved out of reach and knelt between her parted thighs. He trailed his fingertips across her abdomen, exploring the taut, tremoring surface. When she reached for him again, he gently brushed her hands aside.

"Relax, Maggie."

She laughed softly, then asked, "How?"

Noah chuckled as he smoothed his fingertips through the pale silk nest that shielded her secrets at the top of her thighs. She trembled, the intimacy of his touch sending a moan whispering past her lips.

He leaned down, his mouth following the trail of his fingertips. She caught her breath, Noah's seductive exploration of her body stilling the beating of her heart for a long moment. His tenderness was such a new experience that she nearly wept.

He moved lower still, gathering her hips between his hands as his mouth settled over her. She whimpered, her body going momentarily rigid with shock as he traced the delicate seam of her femininity with the tip of his tongue, then delved deeply into the humid folds of her body. He treated her like a feast then, his lips and teeth and tongue tantalizing, shockingly invasive, and seductively inquisitive as he satisfied his hunger for her womanly essence.

She surrendered, trust and love for Noah mingling within her and inspiring a brand of confidence in a man that she'd never known before. Awash in sensation and very nearly mindless with pleasure, Maggie's climax happened with no warning whatsoever. She cried out, coming up from the bed in surprise, her shock apparent as her insides suddenly clenched, then shimmered at length like a brilliant fireworks display on a hot summer night.

Noah urged her back into a reclining position. She possessed no strength, her bones like soft putty, her flesh still tingling with sensation, her entire body quaking. Noah soothed her with gentle hands. She eventually caught her breath and opened her eyes, and, although still somewhat disoriented, she realized that she'd never before experienced such stunningly intimate generosity.

She reached out to him, invitation in her eyes, willingness in her heart. She wanted more from him, wanted to feel the jutting power of his body buried deeply within her own. The extent of her hunger for possession startled her for a moment, but it failed to deter her as she tried to tug him closer.

He deflected her hands and moved up her body at his own pace, pressing hot kisses and tender bites and then additional stinging kisses to every centimeter of skin he encountered. Maggie gripped his shoulders when he paused over her breasts, savoring the muscular strength beneath her fingertips. Amazement flowed through her when she saw the appreciation in his eyes.

"You're exquisite, Maggie-mine."

She cupped the side of his face, not certain what to say, but too happy to contradict him or to tell him that she'd never loved anyone more than she loved him now, never felt such desire for a man in her entire life. She felt cherished, the newness of the experience overcoming her with emotion and closing her throat to speech. Tears filled her eyes, but she blinked them away.

His hands were possessive as he cupped her breasts, and she savored the uniqueness of being wanted solely for herself. Leaning over her, Noah swirled the tip of his tongue across an already distended nipple. She arched into his mouth, arousal sparkling like polished diamonds strewn across the landscape of her senses. Pleasure unfurled within her like an endless, brightly colored banner, the shades so brilliant that she felt momentarily blinded. Breathless and shaking within seconds, she gripped his upper arms.

Noah shifted to her other breast, suckling her, drawing her so deeply into his mouth that she felt on the verge of being consumed. He simultaneously smoothed his fingertips down her midriff and across her belly, pausing at the tangled silk at the juncture of her thighs. Dipping two fingers into her moist heat, he rhythmically delved into the tight channel while also lightly pressing the heel of his hand against the pearl of delicate flesh that topped her sex.

Maggie jerked up from the bed, a low moan coming from her throat as another sweet, hot sensory storm began to overtake her. She quickened inside. Noah chose that moment to move over her, settle between her parted thighs, and penetrate her. The shocking feel of his hard flesh as he surged into her body served to heighten the sensations already overtaking her. He repeatedly plunged into her. She unraveled with a sudden, shocked scream, then went spinning into some cosmic oblivion thanks to the force and length of the powerful release that claimed her.

Noah inhaled the stunned sounds she made, and he savored both the bite of her fingernails as she gripped his hips and the near violent quaking of her body. He rode out her storm, tantalized by the fluttering interior network of nerves and tiny muscles that clutched at his hard flesh and nearly sent him on the same quest for completion.

He fought for control as she quivered beneath him, but he remained imbedded within the dark, wet heat of her body. He gave her time to regain her awareness of him, his tender words blending with the uneven cadence of her breathing during the moments that followed.

He began to move inside of her yet again, testing the receptivity of her body. Maggie uttered a soft sound of surprise as she opened her eyes. Noah, still positioned over her, anchored her head between his hands. She looked faintly dazed, but only until he started to rock more purposefully back and forth against her.

"This is heaven," she whispered as she matched his rhythm and undulated beneath him.

"You're heaven." His body craved release, but his desire to thoroughly please her guarded his control.

Maggie tugged his head down and claimed his lips. Her tongue darted into his mouth while her fingertips smoothed over his back, then shifted down to his hips. His thrusts intensified, and she answered each one with jolting little upturns of her pelvis.

Noah groaned, the innocently sensual instincts of the woman in his arms shattering his good intentions. His respiration grew ragged. His appetite for her spiked out of control, his patience and his restraint finally devastated. He gathered her close, his intense need for fruition evident when he deepened their kiss and duplicated with his lips and tongue the driving force of the lower regions of their bodies.

Tension built inside them, mutual need guiding their journey.

Maggie called out his name as she began to spiral out of control. Noah responded to her plaintive cry and the feverish pitch of her arousal.

Urgency slammed into him like a blow from a well-aimed fist. She jerked suddenly, triggering first her own and then his release. They climaxed together, the splintering impact like exploding dynamite.

Spent and gasping for breath, they collapsed in a tangle of limbs. Sleep claimed them, but only for a little while.

EIGHT

Slender fingertips flowed in slow motion across Noah's hair-roughened upper thighs, lightly massaging the muscular surface. Warm breath followed, then the press of lips that left delicate little kisses in their wake.

Pleasure rippled through Noah's body and simmered in his veins. He exhaled, the sound rich with shock, but he didn't move. In the minutes that followed, he barely managed to breathe.

Maggie knelt between his muscular thighs, aware that Noah was awake and responsive to her touch. He said nothing, though, and she was secretly relieved. She knew she didn't excel at bedroom patter, but he'd made such sweet love to her a few hours ago, she wanted nothing more than to give him the same gift.

She combed her fingertips through the dense nest of coarse hair that surrounded his maleness, stroking, exploring, getting accustomed to this new freedom. He pulsed with life, as though to summon her touch. She accepted the summons and clasped him between gentle hands.

Lowering her head, she experimented by flicking her tongue across the velvet-smooth tip, then slowly trailed it down the length of him. The low moan that burst from him made her pause, though, and she flashed a glance in his direction.

"Don't stop."

She heard the raw need that resonated in his voice. It encouraged and inspired her. She grew braver, her hold on him snugging, the sweep of her tongue more encompassing and more confident as she caressed him intimately. She closed her mouth around him, measuring the thickness of his shaft when she surrounded him with her lips. When she took more of him into her mouth, licking him with long swipes of her tongue, she absently registered his shock by the way in which his entire body tensed and tremored.

Her hesitation fled then, because she realized that it didn't matter that she had never done this before. Nothing mattered, other than turning the tables on Noah and returning his generosity.

She felt empowered by what they'd already shared, not just by the need to express the depth of her feelings for him. She tasted and savored the mingling flavors of their mutual passion from their earlier encounter, then breathed in the muskiness that accompanied it. Taste and scent melded and became a powerful aphrodisiac to her senses.

Maggie gave, instinct, love, and desire guiding her and overriding any lingering concern that he would realize how new she was to this kind of intimacy. And as she gave, she discovered the sweetly torturous pleasure of receiving as her own body softened and liquified in response to him.

She grew bolder with every passing minute. She became more aroused, as well. Noah shuddered, then stiffened beneath her mouth and hands. Her touch became increasingly erotic as she sucked him deeply into her mouth, simultaneously skimming her hands over his abdomen and thighs. She felt the press of his erection against the back of her throat. She slowly withdrew, using the smooth edges of her teeth on him, then repeated the caress.

She moved in concert with the subtle upthrust of his hips in the minutes that followed, memorizing the warmth of his skin, delighting in the interplay of bunching muscles just below the surface as she stroked him, glorying in his response. She heard the sounds—rawly erotic and wholly masculine—that passed his lips before he could bite them back. She loved him with everything she possessed, heart and mind and body committed to tantalizing him to the edge of madness as she swirled her tongue over his hard flesh, then alternately sucked and sipped at him until she sensed that he was ready to burst.

Noah suddenly reared up from the bed, seized her under the arms, and dragged her up his body. He held her suspended above him. "You're killing me, woman."

She gave him a shy look. "Was that a complaint?"

He shook his head in amazement. "Hardly."

She smiled and flowed across him, her pelvis nuzzling his groin so intimately when she locked him between her upper thighs that he drew in a tortured-sounding breath. "You *are* hard," she whispered against the side of his neck.

"And you're a tease."

"Am I?" She pressed a kiss to his chin, then another one for good measure. "Credit yourself as my inspiration."

His hands found her hips. He lifted her, then invaded her. She knew that no other word could have adequately described his sudden penetration. She gasped, the sound reflecting the starkness of the pleasure she felt as it rushed out of her. He shifted her so that she sat astride him. She leaned slightly forward, her breasts swaying with invitation as she plunged her fingers into the pelt of dark hair that covered his chest.

Settling more firmly over him, she kneaded the muscles beneath her fingers and rocked her hips back and forth. She exhaled shakily, her eyes falling half closed, her skin flushing thanks to the steadily escalating arousal that scalded her senses and seemed intent on ravaging every centimeter of her body.

Noah ground his jaws together for a moment before he asked, "What are you thinking right now?"

She didn't have to carefully consider her response, she realized. This was Noah, and he accepted her for herself. Her feeling of liberation from the past provided her with immense satisfaction, and she enjoyed the simple process of saying, "That I want to share everything with you."

His body reacted to her remark, his maleness flexing deep inside of her.

Maggie shivered ever so delicately, then smiled, a sweetly seductive smile as old as time.

"You will," he vowed roughly as he covered her breasts with his hands, plucked at her nipples with skillful fingers, and surged up into her tight heat.

"I liked tasting us," she whispered almost dreamily as desire steamed like a freight train through her veins.

Noah groaned, shock in his heated gaze as he looked at her. The hands gripping her hips tightened even more. He set the pace then, hard, relentless, and so utterly scintillating that she fought for every breath she took.

Finding her rhythm almost immediately, Maggie met his piercing thrusts with tight circular counterthrusts of her own. She kept her eyes locked on his face the entire time. Their joining scorched her soul and seared her heart. Small cries spilled from her. Her body began to tighten into itself, and she started to feel light-headed.

Convulsions that matched the thunder in the pulse points of her body claimed her, sent her reeling into a space made up of explosive starbursts. She cried out, Noah's name a scream of shock sending him over the edge. He slammed upward, impaling her as his life force jetted hotly into the clenching interior of her body.

She trembled in the throes of the shattering volatility of a sustained climax, but she experienced another sensation, as well. Dizziness. Maggie blindly reached out, seeking stability and balance as her body continued to violently quake in response to Noah's throbbing release.

It was like imploding and smothering at the same time, she realized as she succumbed to the forces that seized control of her. She moaned an inarticulate protest, then slumped forward.

Despite his own tumultuous orgasm, Noah's experience told him instantly what had just happened to Maggie. He grabbed her as she slid forward, caught her as she fainted for the first time in her life.

Their bodies still joined, he cradled her close and shifted onto his side. As he held her, he allowed himself the luxury of speaking the words he'd longed to say to her for many years, but only because he knew she wouldn't hear them this time. "I love you, Maggie-mine. I will always love you."

She opened her eyes a short while later and found herself anchored against the hard wall of Noah's chest. "What happened?"

He smiled down at her as she shifted onto her back. "You fainted."

"I don't faint," she said, sounding emphatic and a little annoyed.

"Well, you did. Maybe I inspired that too."

She remembered the smothering sensation. She also remembered feeling that her climax seemed destined to go on forever. "I couldn't catch my breath."

"How do you feel now?"

Shocked. Amazed. Happy. Safe. Wanted. She felt all the things she'd always dreamed of feeling in the arms of the man she loved. "Appreciated," she finally said as she met his gaze. *I love you, Noah, but will you ever love me?*

"You are appreciated, more than I think you realize."

Emotion suddenly swamped her. She resisted the tears, but they filled her eyes anyway. She despaired for a moment about her absence of control, but the compassion she saw in his eyes eased her embarrassment. "You were worth waiting for, Noah," she said softly.

He nearly crushed her as he embraced her. "It was a long wait, though. A very long wait."

The phone rang at dawn. Noah grabbed it on the second ring. Sitting up, he swung his legs over the side of the bed and switched on the night table lamp. Maggie shifted sleepily beside him, her body partially covered by a sheet.

"Sutton," he said into the receiver, then paused to listen to the caller. He shook his head, his displeasure with the words he heard evident in the expression on his face.

It's too soon, he thought, much too soon for this to happen. Maggie's not ready for this.

"Bill, I can't get away right now. You'll have to handle it."

He listened intently for another minute or so. He felt the slide of Maggie's fingertips up his back. Turning, he watched her lift her head from the pillow and peer at him. He took her hand. After pressing a kiss to her fingertips, he stroked the center of her palm with the tip of his tongue. She smiled at him, and her eyes sparkled with pleasure.

"Why didn't you say that in the first place, Bill? If she's just gone into labor, you need to be with her. Put Sergei on the phone. I'll deal with him."

Awake now, Maggie freed herself and shoved several pillows against the head of the bed. She sank back against them. As she drew the sheet up over her naked body, she watched Noah, her expression far less animated now. She remembered another man named Sergei, and she couldn't help thinking of his careless cruelty and the destruction he'd wrought.

"Good morning," he said tersely. "What's it going to take to resolve this situation, Sergei?"

Silence stretched as he listened to the man. A muscle ticked high in his jaw. "Let's cut to the bottom line here, Sergei. Tell the people at State that I've agreed to mediate. I want all parties here within ten hours. State will handle the transportation details for you. And Sergei, say yes now, because I won't make this offer twice."

Noah waited a moment, then said, "Fine." He slammed the phone down and muttered a foul word. Maggie's surprise at his flaring temper showed in her expressive features when he looked at her.

"Trouble?" she asked.

Noah nodded. "Major trouble. The old eastern bloc countries are coming apart at the seams. It's a political powder keg. There are too many factions carrying weapons, people are going hungry, and innocent children are dying."

"How'd you get involved? This doesn't sound like your usual cup of tea, Noah. Trade agreements are more your specialty."

"They are, but the president leaned on me pretty heavily, so my firm took on the confidential negotiations. Washington can't sanction the meetings in any official manner until the UN comes through with a resolution the Ambassador's been working on for several months."

Her uneasiness returned. "They're coming here?"

He nodded. "I don't intend to go there."

"And *there* is . . . ?"

"Washington. Rostov's like a bull in a china shop, and he's heading one of the delegations. It makes more sense to get him out of there so that we can get this situation sorted out away from the media. They've already figured out that something's going on."

She reacted swiftly, the name Rostov the only catalyst she needed to vacate Noah's bed. She slid free of the sheets, and scrambled to her feet.

"What's got you moving so fast?"

Maggie sensed that he already knew the answer to his question. She refused to meet his gaze as she searched for her panties and bra. "I need a shower."

"Want your back scrubbed?" he asked, an edge in his voice as he got to his feet.

Maggie straightened after rescuing her discarded clothing from the floor. She pulled on her T-shirt before she answered him. "No, thanks. You probably have things you need to do. Don't worry about me."

He stepped in front of her as she headed for the bathroom. She started to sidestep him, then recognized the futility of such behavior. If Noah wanted to stop her, he would. Correction. He already had.

"You're running, Maggie."

She held on to her temper, but she couldn't find a cure for the panic that was eating away at the edges of the confidence she'd reclaimed during the previous month. "No, I'm not. Just trying to clear the area. You have a lot of work ahead of you."

"I know Rostov's a problem for you. I also know he was a key player in Randall's fall from grace, but most of the people coming in on that plane use Russian or German as secondary languages. Rostov's the only one who's fluent in English. I need a translator, Maggie," he said bluntly. "I need you. Will you help me?"

She went rigid with shock at his thoughtless disregard for the devastation made of her life by people like Rostov. "How dare you?"

"I asked you a direct question." He sounded hard and ruthless.

"Go to hell!"

"I've been there, dammit, and so have you."

"I'm not going back."

"Don't run. Take a stand. Here. Now. You owe it to yourself," he insisted as he grabbed her wrists and jerked her to a spot between his naked thighs. Oblivious to his state of undress, Noah watched her through narrowed eyes. "You owe it to us."

"Have them bring their own translators or call

the language school at Monterey. There are plenty of qualified people around."

"I want you," he insisted.

"I'd be rejected out of hand, and you know it."

"I won't permit that to happen."

"That's your ego talking. Besides, you have no control over other people's reactions to me, Noah. None whatsoever, despite what you seem to think."

"This is my ball game, and the rules are mine to make."

She glared at him, even though she had to make a concerted effort to ignore the impact the closeness of his muscular body was having on her. "I'm not part of the team, so don't you dare make rules for me."

"That isn't what I said, and you know it."

"Rostov helped to destroy my life once, and I don't plan to give him a second opportunity."

"How?"

"How what?" she snapped.

"How did he destroy your life?"

She exhaled in frustration. "I'm certain you already know the details, so why rehash it now?"

"Tell me," he grated.

"Rostov gave a press conference the morning after Randall's body was found. He told the entire world that I'd been a coconspirator. He ruined my credibility in the diplomatic community, and he made it impossible for me to obtain a classified clearance so that I could continue to work as a translator." She tried to tug free of him, but his grip only tightened. "Let go of me, Noah. You're being cruel. No one, not even you, has the right to insult or humiliate me ever again."

"Randall Hartley was guilty of treason, not you. It's time to confront the people who linked you to the scandal. I've known since last year that Rostov was one of Randall's coconspirators, which is why I loathe dealing with the bastard, but I have no choice right now."

She lifted her chin, pride making her adamant. "I do."

"Use your head. By implicating you, Rostov took attention away from himself, but everyone knew he was Randall's puppeteer. Like all good government employees everywhere, he did what was expedient. The situation's simple. He's a survivor. He's also as slick as they come. Maggie, the bottom line here is simple: He gets to live free as a bird while also representing his government in a new capacity. You, on the other hand, are about to readmit yourself to that bloody prison of yours. Makes a whole hell of a lot of sense, doesn't it?" he demanded sarcastically.

She shuddered, her memories so weighted down with humiliation and anguish that she felt as though someone had encased her body in lead. "You expect too much of me."

"What I expect is common sense and a well-thought-out offense. I also expect you to reclaim your entire life with both hands, or we cannot move forward in this relationship. I'll be by your side every step of the way. I want a future with you, Maggie, but I need you to be a part of every facet of my life, not just a bed partner. If you don't face your demons once and for all, we're doomed. I cannot and will not abandon my career because you aren't willing to defend your own integrity. You were innocent, for God's sake. Why the hell don't you act like it?"

"Let go of me," she said with as much dignity as she could muster.

He released her, although his reluctance was evident. "Don't do this, Maggie. There's no point to it."

"Good-bye, Noah. You've been a great refresher course on hidden agendas and manipulation."

Head held high, Maggie walked out of the master suite. She paused on the landing at the top of the staircase to step into her jeans and put on her T-shirt. She stuffed her underwear into her purse once she got to the kitchen, then walked outside to her car.

The dawn broke across the Pacific coastline as she numbly drove home. Although sick to her stomach and sick at heart, she didn't cry. For a little while she wanted to, but then she saw the wisdom of keeping her emotions under lock and key.

Protecting herself, she'd already discovered, was far easier to do when she felt clearheaded. Maggie just wished she'd been wise enough to exercise caution before she'd given Noah the power to shatter her dreams and break her heart.

NINE

Maggie's emotional numbness persisted for several hours. Exhausted from too little sleep, she got into bed, but she abandoned the effort after an hour of tossing and turning. She soaked in a hot tub in what turned out to be a vain attempt to relax and clear her mind of the incident with Noah.

While bathing temporarily eased the residual achiness caused by sexual intimacy for the first time in several years, her body still reminded her each time she moved of the ecstasy she'd found in his arms. She dressed for the day and tried housecleaning to distract herself, but what she viewed as flawed judgment on her part for trusting Noah in the first place continued to haunt her until it gave way to the necessity of dealing honestly with their predawn confrontation.

She felt betrayed and used, although she had

to admit to herself that she'd been a willing participant in her own seduction. Still, she harshly chastised herself for being foolish enough to allow Noah the opportunity to manipulate her for his own purposes.

Maggie hated all the negative feelings she had, but she faced them. Evasion and denial were habits from her past, habits she'd vowed not to indulge in ever again.

She longed to believe that Noah hadn't planned all along to try to draw her back into the diplomatic community, but she couldn't. She knew him well enough to realize that he never had just one agenda at any given moment, and she sensed that the issue of her talent as a multilingual translator had been in the back of his mind since day one, just waiting like a tiger to pounce.

Being placed in the position of feeling like a hapless victim angered her. She told herself that she should have guessed his plans for her. After all, they had a history of friendship and emotional intimacy—a history he apparently expected to use as a convenience now that he'd purchased the Carmel estate.

Maggie grudgingly admired his tactics. Outmaneuvering people was pure Noah Sutton. He'd certainly managed the feat with her, she concluded irritably. She couldn't help wondering, though, if his timetable had been slightly off-kilter. She'd sensed his annoyance with the phone call, as though being caught off guard by the necessity of stepping in as mediator during these particular negotiations. He clearly disliked having to deal with Rostov. Maggie finally decided that he'd behaved like a man rushed to the starting gate before completing his preparations for a successful race.

She already knew about his ability to dazzle his opponents at the negotiating table. She didn't feel dazzled, however. What she felt was fury with him and frustration with herself, the latter because she'd permitted her emotions to blind her to the man and his reputation for being ruthlessly single-minded when he set goals for himself.

Loving him made her vulnerable, she realized, but she promised herself that she wouldn't compound the situation by allowing her emotional entanglement with him to make her stupid as well. Feeling trapped and edgy, Maggie left the cottage and drove to the beach in the middle of the afternoon. The warm sun and gentle ocean breezes soothed her in ways that nothing else could.

As she walked and once she settled down sufficiently to think rationally, she searched her heart and her conscience. She loved Noah, and she took responsibility for her decision to make love with him. Blaming him for a conscious choice, she concluded, made absolutely no sense.

She thought, too, about the manner in which she'd dealt with Randall's treason and death three years earlier. She'd cowered in fear and then she'd run, too frightened and too emotionally devastated to do anything else at the time. She hadn't been strong enough in those days to risk riding out the storm of innuendo and ridicule caused by his duplicity.

Maggie knew in her heart that she'd grown and matured in recent years, despite the reclusive manner in which she'd chosen to live. Stronger now, capable of articulating her feelings, and willing to draw boundary lines for those people she admitted into her life, she possessed a new confidence. It was fragile, but she felt a sense of certainty that she could build on it if given the chance.

Take a stand.

You were innocent. Why in hell don't you act like it?

Face your demons. We're doomed if you don't.

I won't give up my career.

I need you.

He'd done everything but call her a coward. She wanted to deny the truth of his words, but in the end she knew she couldn't. Not confronting a man like Rostov was cowardice in its purest form. She owed herself more, Maggie realized as the afternoon sun started to grow hazy and the scent of rain filled the air.

She stumbled to a stop in the sand after another relentless hour of soul-searching, suddenly aware that she deserved the opportunity to publicly reclaim her personhood and her professional reputation. She felt strong enough and more than capable now of defending herself if anyone ever wrongly accused her again.

Maggie decided then to return to the estate, but on her terms and for her own reasons. She intended to make it clear to Rostov that while people and events could be orchestrated, the inner spirit of this particular casualty of his self-serving machinations refused to be vanquished.

Maggie didn't pretend to understand all of Noah's motives, but she promised herself that she would as she resumed her trek down the beach. The breeze cooled, and the threat of rain became a reality. She paused at the water's edge, watching the raindrops disappear into the low surf. Her thoughts remained centered on Noah. Loving him was a separate issue as far as she was concerned, but an issue she needed to deal with. She already knew from experience that love didn't come with a warranty or an instruction manual. She realized, too, that a love that wasn't based on faith and trust and the strength to accept your mate unconditionally was destined for failure.

In spite of his manipulative behavior, she loved Noah deeply. Jarred for a moment by the actual depth of her feelings for him, she recognized that she would always love him. Whether or not he loved her enough to make a permanent commitment to a life together wasn't something she felt compelled to tackle at the moment. For now, she would deal with the career she'd lost and the man who'd devastated her reputation as a woman of integrity.

The rain suddenly intensified. Maggie ran to her car and drove the short distance to her cottage. She changed into her Chanel suit, freshened her makeup, and arranged her hair in a snug French braid. After packing an overnight bag, she made her way through a steady downpour to the estate in Carmel.

The security people at the front gate promptly admitted her, calling her by name. Although somewhat startled by this turn of events, Maggie thanked the armed men and proceeded up the driveway to the main house. She hesitated at the front door, decided against using the key that Noah had given her, and simply knocked.

He answered the door himself, alerted, Maggie assumed, by security of her arrival. "Welcome back."

She stepped inside. "I'm not a coward, in spite of what you implied this morning."

He closed the door, his steady gaze on her as she crossed the foyer. "Your presence proves that."

"You owe me some answers, and I expect to have them once the negotiations are finished."

"Sounds fair."

"Good." She heard a burst of laughter and the sound of voices. "I assume your guests have arrived."

He nodded. "A little while ago."

"They're a few hours ahead of schedule." Maggie shrugged out of her raincoat, handing it and her luggage to a uniformed man who materialized out of nowhere and departed just as quickly. "I'm here to help, if you still want me."

Noah studied her features for several silent moments, then walked toward her. He paused just a few feet from where she stood, his facial expression neutral although his eyes burned with an intensity she didn't understand.

"I want you, Maggie. Very much."

"I won't apologize for what I said to you earlier," she warned him, strengthened by her recognition that, despite her dislike of his methods, this man had cared enough about her to fight for her.

"I don't expect that of you."

"You tried to manipulate me. I suspect that it would have happened eventually, because I know you well enough to realize that you don't do anything without thinking it through in advance."

"This situation wasn't supposed to happen quite so soon," he conceded.

"You were hoping to build my confidence a little more before you sprang this kind of a challenge on me, weren't you?"

"Yes. I meant it when I said I needed you, and not just in my bed."

"I believe you."

"You sound like your old self again."

She smiled wryly. "This is the upgraded and much improved version of the old me."

"Will you trust me?"

"I'm here, aren't I, Noah?" She hesitated briefly, then said, "I felt like you'd jerked the proverbial rug out from under my feet this morning. I didn't know how to cope with it or you when it happened. But I do now."

"You came back, so you must've stopped running."

"I'm not a coward," she said a second time. "I needed to work this through on my own, though, not be managed into submission by someone with good intentions."

He had the good grace to look guilty. "I never thought you were a coward."

"Yes, you did, although you might not have used the specific word." She paused, weighing her next comment before she spoke again. "I needed the last few years to heal. I had a right to take the time for myself."

"I agree."

"If there's a next time, don't surprise me," she cautioned.

He moved closer.

She felt the heat generated by his strong body. Desire for him stole into her veins and flirted with her senses, making her want to take the final step to close the space that separated their bodies. She remembered then what his hands had felt like when he'd touched her the previous night. The images that played through her mind were both sensual and seductive. She sank her teeth into her lower lip, trapping the moan that threatened to break free of her when she saw the desire that darkened his hazel eyes.

Heat moved sluggishly through her bloodstream, sending need tremoring through her entire body. She wanted him, in spite of a houseful of people and the emotional gauntlet she'd just run. She exhaled shakily, craving his touch now almost as much as she craved air to breathe.

His gaze swept her face. *I want you,* his eyes said. "You always did hate surprises."

She sensed the depth of his hunger for her, felt his need as he reached for her. It brought to mind the intense passion they'd shared before a ringing phone had disrupted their first night together. "Try to remember that in the future, please. I won't be managed or coerced, not even by you."

He curved his hands over her shoulders, slowly drawing her forward. Maggie forgot all about foreign dignitaries and armed guards in the moments that followed. Her world shrank as she stared up at Noah. She felt what she'd always wanted to feel when the man she loved touched her—the heavy beat of his heart in his fingertips.

"I need you, Maggie. I . . ."

"What's that woman doing here?" demanded a man that Maggie didn't recognize. His heavily accented voice told her of his heritage, though, and she gave him a direct look.

Noah whirled around and pierced Rostov's

aide with a hard look. "Ms. Holden is our translator, Leonid."

"I recognize this woman," he exclaimed, his alarm apparent. "She is not suitable. Send her away. Sergei will be outraged by her presence."

Maggie's chin lifted, her features filled with defiance.

Noah's expression turned glacial. "Sergei can go straight to hell, Leonid. Ms. Holden stays. We're a team, and you're on my turf now."

A burly man strolled out of the dining room. His Armani suit and silk tie served to emphasize his air of self-importance. His girth made a statement about his self-indulgent personality. "What's the holdup, Noah?"

Maggie stiffened the instant she spotted Rostov.

"There's no holdup, Sergei. Ms. Holden was late in arriving."

Sergei studied her through narrowed eyes. Maggie couldn't help thinking that he probably had countless mental photos to sort through before he could identify all the people he'd harmed. She waited while he located her in his personal catalog of abuse.

"I remember you," he finally remarked, contempt in his tone. "You're Hartley's widow."

Maggie bristled, but she held her temper. "You have an excellent memory. I also remember you, Mr. Rostov. I particularly recall the press conference you held following Randall's death."

The man's gaze narrowed. He flashed a look of outrage in Noah's direction.

"You're on your own, Sergei."

"Despite what you said to the media three years ago, I wasn't guilty of treason. In fact, I was totally innocent of any wrongdoing against my government, Mr. Rostov. You owe me an apology for your lies." She didn't expect him to provide one, of course, but she felt liberated by the freedom of simply articulating her expectations to a pompous creature like Rostov. The fact that he looked mildly apoplectic provided Maggie with a large measure of satisfaction.

The diplomat stiffened, clearly unaccustomed to anyone making demands on him. Ruddy color suffused his face. "What is this nonsense, Noah?"

"The lady is perfectly capable of speaking for herself, so address your questions to her."

Maggie held her ground, encouraged by Noah's ability to support her without feeling compelled to run to her rescue. "The lady in question dislikes liars, Mr. Rostov, but she is a skilled translator. You are fortunate to have her at these meetings."

With that said, she crossed the foyer, deposited her purse on a lamp table, checked her hair in the mirror above it, and then walked into the formal dining room. Although shaking inside from the confrontation, she took pride in the poise she displayed.

Maggie paused just inside the doorway, listening to Noah and Rostov as she perused the gathered dignitaries, some of whom she recognized, indulging in a buffet and cocktails provided by their host. In the past, she would never have challenged the honor of a diplomat or provoked a scene. She'd always been the soul of discretion and good manners. This time, however, she felt justified in taking a stand.

"You tempt fate, Sutton."

"The meetings will not proceed without her. The clearances have been obtained."

"The woman is impudent. She insulted me."

"It seems a small price to pay, considering what you did to her."

"I won't tolerate—"

Noah interrupted, his voice harsh as he said, "You will tolerate anything she says to you. You deserve far worse for slandering her reputation. Now," he said, sounding calmer, "shall we get to work, or shall I have you flown back to Washington? I can always call your government and explain that you've refused to participate. When I spoke to the premier this morning, he made it clear that he wants these negotiations brought to a prompt and successful conclusion. He's counting on the foreign aid promised to him by the president, but he knows the funds won't be forthcoming if you fail."

Rostov shifted uneasily.

Leonid, the erstwhile aide, sputtered ineffectually, then fell silent after a quelling glance from his superior.

Noah looked as though his features had been carved from stone as he stared at the man that diplomatic necessity now forced him to deal with in his own home. As he waited for Rostov's reply, he silently promised himself that he would lease appropriate office space within the week. He wanted his home to be an island of serenity in the future. He just hoped that he wouldn't be the only inhabitant.

Noah glanced at Maggie, his expression softening as he watched her greet one of the diplomats in the dining room. He had never been more proud of her. Nor had he ever loved her more. He knew they still had a great deal left to resolve, but handling delegates who were still sniping at each other like children across a backyard fence had to be their first priority.

People were dying, and Noah knew Maggie well enough to realize that she shared his conviction that that particular reality had to take precedence over all others for the time being. The fact that she would be at his side, partnered with him as they worked for a settlement of the bloody regional dispute, gave him hope that there would be time later to persuade her to consider a shared future.

Rostov cleared his throat, his usual bluster notably absent.

Noah peered at him, his demeanor chilly. "What's the verdict?"

"We shall proceed. I am here to serve my premier and my people."

"That's what I assumed," Noah remarked dryly.

He ushered Rostov and his aide into the dining room. After speaking to a State Department official who intercepted him a few steps into the room, Noah made his way to Maggie and drew her aside.

"Thank you for backing me up when I spoke to Rostov."

"I believe in you, Maggie-mine. I always have, and I always will."

She smiled. "If I had any remaining doubts about that, I resolved them a few minutes ago."

"Are you all right?" he asked.

"I'm better than I've been in a long time."

"Then let's get in gear. We have a lot of issues to resolve before we can get these people back on that plane."

She grinned, laughter in her eyes.

He warned, "Call me Fearless Leader, and I'll turn you over my knee right now."

Her grin widened. "My skirt's too short to risk that kind of a threat."

"Lucky for you." He traced the curve of her cheek with his fingertips. "I'm proud of you," he told her, his voice containing the kind of intimacy usually reserved for the bedroom.

"Ditto," she whispered.

"Mr. Sutton?"

Noah turned to find the State Department representative he'd spoken to a few minutes earlier at his elbow. "Yes?"

"Our people have secured the meeting room, sir. We can get underway now."

"Thank you." He glanced at Maggie. "Ready?"

She nodded.

Together they led the assembled diplomats and their aides to the negotiating table.

Twenty-four hours later, Noah suggested that the delegates adjourn to their respective corners for a cooling-off period. Tempers had reached flash point. Fatigue and long-standing contentiousness among the adversaries facing each other across the negotiating table had taken a notable toll on everyone involved.

Maggie gratefully took the opportunity to excuse herself from the fray. She stopped in the kitchen, fixed a snack from the buffet arranged by the caterer Noah had hired, and then was escorted upstairs to one of the guest rooms by a security team member. She didn't question the escort or the assignment of her room. The process simply reminded her of the protocol that had once dominated her life when she'd worked for Noah.

After satisfying her need for nourishment, she

bathed, put on her robe, and stretched out atop the bed. She knew better than to settle in for the night, because the meetings would very likely resume in just a few hours. A nap would have to do for the time being.

A knock sounded at her door, jarring her just as she dozed off. "Yes?"

"It's Noah."

"Come in," she said as she shifted up against the pillows stacked at the head of the bed.

"Connor said you were in here. Did I wake you?" he asked as he stepped into the room and closed the door behind him.

"Not really. I never sleep well during these marathon sessions."

Noah approached the bed and sat on the edge of it.

"You look tired," she remarked as she scanned his features.

He shrugged. "I'll catch up later."

"How do you think we're doing?"

"Better than I expected, in spite of no sleep and short tempers."

"Rostov certainly enjoys provoking his fellow delegates."

Noah nodded. "Several of them have figured him out, though. With a little luck, he'll be the catalyst that brings the other factions together."

"The phones must be busy."

He smiled. "There are two communications trailers parked behind the guest cottages. State had the local Army base send them down. Everyone's checking in with their respective governments." He glanced at his watch. "We'll start up again in four or five hours."

Maggie reached out and trailed her fingertips over the top of his free hand. She felt the warmth of his skin and suddenly craved the feel of his hands on her body. She shivered and looked away, knowing in her heart that she had to deny herself.

"Talk to me," he said quietly.

She shook her head. "Not now."

He exhaled, the sound harsh in the still room. "You've been very patient with me."

"I've tried."

"You've succeeded, Noah."

"I want you."

"I want you, too, but sometimes wanting isn't enough," she said gently.

"What are you trying to say?"

She searched his features for understanding. "I'm not altogether certain yet, so let's save this conversation for another time."

He released her hand and pushed to his feet. Maggie watched him cross the room, his destination the door.

"I'll have someone wake you in a few hours."

Maggie got up from the bed, pulling closed the gaping lapels of her robe as she followed Noah. He turned and looked at her, his hand on the doorknob, his expression more troubled than she'd ever seen it. She hesitated a few feet from him, although hungry for the feel of his arms around her. She wanted to verbalize the depth of her feelings for him, but the words remained locked in her heart. Telling Noah that she'd fallen in love with him wasn't something she intended to risk. She sensed that such a statement would serve no useful purpose other than compromising Noah and making her even more emotionally vulnerable than she'd already become during their time together.

"You're pulling away from me, aren't you?"

She met his hard gaze and reluctantly nodded, the admission a costly one. "I don't have any other choice right now."

"We always have choices, Maggie."

She smiled sadly, aware of the one she might be forced to make for both their sakes. "You're right, but sometimes they hurt."

He drove his fingers through his dense, short-cropped hair. "You're not making any sense."

"Could I have a hug?" she asked, ignoring his remark.

His hand fell to his side. "Dammit, Maggie!"

She stepped up to him. "Was that a yes?"

He jerked her into his arms, his frustration with her obvious. She clung to him, understanding his inner conflict because it matched her own. He held her for several silent minutes, and she felt the strength of his desire for her in the fierce pounding of his heart against her breasts and the strength flooding his loins. She trembled, unable to stop herself from responding to him when he found her mouth and claimed it. His claiming would have felt like an angry assault from any other man, but to Maggie it was simply a reflection of the desire scalding her veins and readying the lower region of her body for his possession.

He deepened their kiss, his hunger explosive and voracious as he plunged his tongue into her mouth and scoured the interior. Maggie responded with equal hunger, her hands skimming his shoulders, then locking at the back of his neck as she writhed against his hard body.

He gripped her hips, grinding himself into the natural cradle of her upper thighs. Inflamed by his movement, she ached almost painfully for the driving force of his passion. She wanted him so desperately in the moments that followed that emotions too diverse to label rose up inside of her, swamped her fragile control, and finally brought tears to her eyes.

Noah drew back suddenly. "I can taste your tears," he said roughly.

She tried to blink them away, but they sparkled on her lower lashes, then trickled down her cheeks. She stared at him, unable to find the right words, fearful of hurting him, aware more now than ever before of the anguish she courted just being in his arms. She struggled to get free, chastising herself for being so self-indulgent. The arms around her tightened. She abandoned her efforts, telling herself to settle down because she was simply making things more stressful for them both by squirming against his aroused body.

"Tell me what's wrong. I love you, Maggie-mine. There's nothing we can't solve together. Nothing."

Shock momentarily paralyzed her. Panic followed. She started to struggle again.

Noah scooped her up against his chest and smoothed her legs around his hips. He took her to the bed, tumbling her back across it before he followed her down. Crouched over her, he studied her through narrowed eyes.

"You don't believe me, do you?"

"You don't lie," she gasped.

"I know you aren't in love with me, but we can make this work."

How could he not know how she felt about him? Maggie wondered, suddenly limp with the shock that reverberated through her.

Two sharp knocks sounded on the bedroom door.

They stared at each other.

Noah muttered a curse.

She felt her heart stutter to a brief stop in her chest. "It might be important," Maggie managed to whisper.

He nodded and shifted to a seated position beside her. Noah exhaled, the sound so raw that her insides hurt.

"Miss Holden?" a voice called out.

"Who is it?" she asked, sounding composed

even though she doubted that she'd ever feel that way again.

"Connor, ma'am. I'm . . ." He paused and cleared his throat. "I'm sorry to disturb you, but I need to locate Mr. Sutton. The president wants to speak to him."

She flashed a glance at Noah, ignored the possibility for gossip that her reply would foster, and said, "He'll be right with you."

Noah got to his feet. "We're not finished with this, Maggie. You were right about one thing. We can't have a decent conversation until we're alone."

She turned onto her side, drawing her legs up, as he crossed the room. Desire still hummed within her body, and her emotions felt flayed. "You'd better go. I'll be down later."

"I'm not giving up on you, Maggie," he announced in a tone of voice she recognized all too well. "Not ever."

It was the voice, she realized, of a man unprepared to relinquish the goal that he'd set for himself. Sighing, Maggie watched him yank open the bedroom door and then disappear from sight. She remained in bed, but she didn't sleep thanks to her stunned emotions and conflicted thoughts.

TEN

The negotiations resumed that evening. The forty hours that followed tested the mettle of everyone involved. Partial agreements, which reminded Maggie of the pieces of a complex puzzle, were achieved. Periodically, though, one or more of the participants backpedaled. Tempers predictably exploded, and the delegates often found themselves in the position of jump-starting the process all over again, but only after they calmed themselves on the heels of a reminder from their host of their responsibilities.

As she watched Noah guide the men and women at the negotiating table in his role as mediator, Maggie appreciated both his ability to lead and his steely determination to hammer out a comprehensive settlement that reinforced the intrinsic value of human life. She knew her love for him colored her opinion of him, but she noticed admiration and grudging respect in the faces of the delegates whenever he addressed the group.

While she trusted her own instincts more and more as the hours lengthened, she also took her cues from Noah, as she had so many times in the past. She asserted herself when the necessity arose by shepherding overstressed participants to the coffee urn for a few moments of idle conversation. She escorted several aides through the estate's garden during one decompression period under the watchful and unexpectedly admiring eyes of the security personnel patrolling the estate. She fielded the language shifts that occurred with a dexterity that seemed to surprise many of the delegates. She even earned two offers of employment, both of which she declined with a polite smile.

Although several delegates, especially those aligned with Rostov, cast uneasy glances at her whenever they thought she wasn't paying attention to them, she felt more confident than she had in several years. She also felt a sense of personal liberation from the dark cloud of innuendo and suspicion that had hung over her since Randall's death, and she gave Noah partial credit for the strides she'd made.

Friend, ally, and lover, he'd given of himself in ways that she still found astonishing. She didn't plan to pursue work as a translator in the future, although she hadn't revealed her decision to him yet. Aside from Noah, no one else could be expected to ignore the reality of her past, especially a scandal caused by treason and the difficulty she would always have of obtaining classified clearances. It was enough, she told herself, that she felt pride in her abilities, the kind of pride that no one could ever rob her of again. She considered the reclamation of her pride a resounding punctuation mark on the loneliness she'd endured in recent years.

Maggie segued effortlessly between her dual roles as translator and unofficial hostess. She felt Rostov's consistent hostility, but she dismissed him and his antagonistic attitude. She felt empowered by her handling of their confrontation at the start of the negotiations, because it had allowed her to see his shallowness, put him in proper emotional perspective, and keep him there. To do otherwise, she knew, would have endangered her credibility and compromised her professional demeanor, and she summarily refused to give anyone that kind of power over her.

As Noah had predicted, the majority of the delegates joined forces against Rostov and maneuvered him into a position of conceding on several points of contention. His aide, Leonid, donned an expression of almost comical dismay that intensified with every passing hour. Maggie worked hard not to laugh out loud at the two men when catfights erupted between them as the negotiations proceeded.

Noah didn't deviate once from his role as presidential envoy. Maggie saw the worry in his eyes when he met her gaze, and she realized that his concern had nothing to do with the work they were doing. They both knew that he couldn't afford to let their uncertain personal situation distract him. From Maggie's vantage point, he remained focused. She knew him too well to be surprised by his self-control and determination.

She deeply regretted the emotional distress she caused him, but she knew that there were tough decisions ahead. Decisions, in particular, that she needed to make, Maggie reflected tiredly, but only once she'd had sufficient sleep to think clearly.

The consummate professional, Noah brought the negotiations to a successful conclusion at the end of the third day. Three secretaries, supplied by the Army and stationed at a bank of computers in the library, produced the finished documents for the agreement hammered out by the exhausted delegates, who were packing for their return flight to Washington and then points east.

Maggie slipped upstairs to her guest room while Noah consulted by secure telephone with the president. She collected her things as all of the delegates and their aides gathered together in the formal living room of the main house to affix their signatures to the agreement on behalf of their respective governments. She knew that champagne toasts would follow the signing and that several official photographs would also be taken to mark the historic event and record the identities of the participants. Waiting limos under tight security would then transport everyone to the airport.

Before she departed the Carmel estate, Maggie spoke privately to Connor, the State Department official. He mentioned that the president wanted Noah in Washington that night, which didn't surprise her. If anything, she felt bittersweet relief. She needed time to assemble her thoughts and get her emotions under control before they saw each other again. After accepting Connor's thanks for her part in the negotiations, she asked him to tell Noah that she'd gone home.

Maggie drove through the darkness, her resolution to catch up on her rest before dealing with her conflicted emotions eclipsed by Noah's presence in her mind. He dominated her thoughts and feelings. She sensed he always would.

Maggie stepped out of her shoes the instant she walked into her cottage. She left her luggage and purse in the living room. Once in her bedroom, she peeled off her clothing, deposited everything in the hamper next to the closet, walked into the bathroom and turned on the shower, and then stepped under the hot spray. The thrumming force of the water helped to ease the tension and fatigue in her body, but it did little to lessen the thoughts flooding her mind.

Noah.

She sighed as she recalled the road of friendship they'd traveled. The emotions and needs he inspired had shocked and frightened her at first, but then she'd recognized an intrinsic truth. Loving Noah had given her the strength to risk feeling again, just as loving him had freed her to be her best. She knew she would never love anyone as she loved him. Her heart ached, but she couldn't escape her certainty that he deserved more than a woman with a permanently tarnished reputation.

Her mind shifted to the passion they'd shared, the vividness of her memories arousing her body almost instantly. She trembled, craving an encore of Noah's generosity as a lover. But on the heels of her desire came the sobering realization that she needed to use her common sense, no matter how difficult the task. Intimacy would make their inevitable parting that much more painful, she knew as she wept silently under the crushing sense of loss she already felt.

I love you, Maggie-mine.

His words echoed in her soul and reverberated in her mind. Stunning words now permanently etched into her heart. Because she knew she couldn't ever risk expressing her true feelings for him, she said them as she stood under the shower, her tears melting on her cheeks as she ducked her head under the water.

"I love you, Noah Sutton, with all my heart. I will always love you, even though I can't have you."

Knowing that Noah had devoted his entire adult life to building a reputation of competence and integrity in the international political arena intensified her desire to protect him in the same way in which he'd protected her with his love and encouragement. His unyielding faith in her courage, which he'd nurtured despite her resistance, had aided her in finding her balance as a woman and as a human being, not just in providing her with the opportunity to confront Rostov.

Although she'd felt manipulated by Noah at the outset of the negotiations, she didn't feel that way any longer. He had been the catalyst that had ended her alienation from a career she'd lost but still valued.

The previous three days had been a refresher course on achievement and the sense of accomplishment she'd experienced in the past when she'd participated in negotiations that forged a successful political compromise. Maggie drew strength, however, from the knowledge that she could use her renewed confidence in herself as a person and as a linguist to benefit her students at the academy.

No one, she decided, could ever be permitted to harm Noah's standing in the diplomatic community, especially not the woman who loved him. And she did love him, more completely and more fiercely than she'd ever loved anyone in her entire life.

Emotionally and physically depleted, Maggie shut off the shower, stepped out of the enclosure, and toweled dry. She didn't bother with a nightgown. She crawled naked into her bed and drew the sheet over her body. Closing her eyes, she listened to Noah's words as they whispered through her mind yet again.

I love you, Maggie-mine.

I know you aren't in love with me, but we can make this work.

I love you. . . .

"I love you, too, Noah," she said as she drifted off.

Maggie slept deeply and dreamlessly for several hours, the fatigue of the previous three days acting like a powerful tranquilizer, but sometime in the middle of the night her subconscious came alive with erotic impulses that made her body throb with desire. She stirred atop the mattress, shifting with sudden restlessness. She pushed aside the sheet that had tangled around her body during the night, then relaxed, her breathing deepening again.

Unexpected sensations roused her once more, swirling languidly throughout her body. She moaned as they undulated through her bloodstream, bringing her to the edge of wakefulness, then tenderly sucking her back into sleep. She sighed, then murmured a name.

The man who loved her heard the sound of his name pass her lips. Moonlight spilled across Maggie's naked form, as though conveying an invitation to touch. He reached out, smoothing his fingertips over her narrow waist, then moving on to the slight curve of her abdomen.

Sprawled on her back, Maggie's thighs parted. A second invitation. Noah didn't resist this one, either. He couldn't. He wanted her with every cell in his body.

He drew in a harsh-sounding breath, the fingers he trailed through the silk at the top of her thighs trembling for a moment. He dipped lower, the tip of one finger following the warm, damp seam of her femininity. Holding his breath to still the groan that rose up inside him, he delved into her heat, his penetration of the soft folds of her flesh filled with tenderness. He felt the tremor that passed through her, and the subsequent tightening of the narrow channel he'd invaded as tiny interior nerves snugged moistly around his finger.

Noah shuddered, desire crashing over him like storm-induced waves as he marveled over the fact that Maggie responded to his touch even in her sleep. Seated beside her on the bed, he watched her, his naked body taut with barely suppressed tension.

She redefined temptation, but she was still asleep, he reminded himself. He withdrew his hand from the silky nest at the top of her thighs. He stroked upward over her torso. Pausing at her breasts, he smoothed a fingertip across the tip of one creamy mound. The mauve bud tightened instantly.

His hunger for her dominating his awareness, he leaned down over her, consciously fighting to control the desire raging through his body, struggling against the impulse that urged him to take her now, to wake her with the plunging force of his need.

He drew her nipple into his mouth, alternately suckling and swirling his tongue around the distended tip. He simultaneously curved his hand around the fullness of her other breast, his fingers shaping, molding. Noah exhaled raggedly, then sucked her deeply into his mouth, feeding on her, desperately trying to satisfy a hunger within his heart that he sensed would never really be appeased, no matter how many times they made love.

Holding back was pure torture, but he endured it. She suddenly arched up into his mouth. He took more of her, licking, biting gently, then sucking so forcefully that she moaned. She didn't pull away, though. He moved to her other breast moments later, still starved for the taste of her. He breathed in the scent of her skin, the sweet, just-washed scent that had been seared into his senses for more than ten years. The fragrance had always haunted him.

He felt her stir beneath his mouth and hands, felt her reach out even though he knew she was still asleep. Her hands slid up his arms, then drifted across his shoulders.

He lifted his head, found her mouth, and traced the shape of her lips with the tip of his tongue. She exhaled, her warm breath like a melodic sigh as it passed her lips. He drank in the sound, then slid his tongue into the heat beyond. She shivered delicately, and her lips parted even more to accept his thrusting tongue.

Without relinquishing her mouth, Noah stretched out beside her. He drew her into his arms, biting back a groan as she turned instinctively into him. Her breasts flattened against his chest, and her legs wove between his. His manhood, already hard, surged against her lower abdomen as she molded herself to him.

Her movements inflamed him, inciting desire that neared flash point almost immediately. He clamped down on the need he felt, although the muscles in his body thrummed and burned and his hands shook as he embraced her.

Maggie went perfectly still just moments later. She surfaced slowly, swimming up from a tangle of sleep and fantasy. Still groggy, she whispered, "Noah?"

He heard her confusion, even understood the reason for it. "I decided not to go to Washington."

She opened her eyes. She looked puzzled, then her expression changed to one of alarm. He understood the reason for her reaction, but he didn't want to hear her say the words. She opened her mouth to speak, but he silenced her with his lips, his hunger for her exploding out of control.

Her hesitation persisted for a second or two, but then she abandoned it and herself to his seductive assault. Relief flooded Noah. He'd felt her attempts to expand the emotional distance between them during the negotiations, and it had taken every shred of self-control in his character not to call a halt to the meetings.

He understood, as well, why Maggie had serious doubts about continuing their relationship. He knew she cared about him, just as he knew that she would never have made love with him without some kind of emotional basis for the intimacy they'd shared. She trusted him. She wasn't in love with him, though, and that undeniable truth hurt in a thousand different ways.

Could she grow to love him? Noah wondered. Would she be willing to give them time to find out?

Somehow, he silently vowed, he would convince her that they had a chance for happiness. Somehow, he intended to persuade her that he possessed enough love for both of them. He planned to use anything and everything in his personal arsenal to bind her to him forever. Anything. He wanted her so much, wanted her with an intensity that bordered on the obsessive. He knew it, but he didn't care, couldn't let himself care. He needed Maggie. Her very existence replenished his neglected heart and soothed his soul. He'd spent too many lonely years without her, and he refused to endure any more if he could avoid it.

Noah rolled suddenly to a position above her, stretching out atop her and tucking her beneath him in a fluid movement without releasing his claim on her mouth. He settled between her thighs, his maleness pulsing against the slick portal of her body.

She undulated beneath him as her fingers dug into his hips, her attempt to get closer testing his control. He bit back a groan, but she shifted yet again, the intimate alignment of their loins causing erotic sensations that were both exquisite and painful.

"I want you now," she gasped.

Need detonated within him. He felt compelled to absorb her into his pores, to stake a claim so undeniable that she wouldn't ever question the wisdom of sharing their lives.

He took her lips with a hunger that defied reason and rationality, intensifying their kiss as he simultaneously thrust into her. She shuddered violently as he possessed her, then brought her legs up to circle his hips, opening herself to him, encouraging the deepest possible penetration of her body. He sank into her as her fingers tangled at his nape, then repeatedly speared into her tight, steamy depths. His groan of disbelief, a reflection of the shocking sense of rightness at having finally found the haven he'd searched for his entire life, echoing through him each time he entered her, mingled with her soft cries of pleasure.

Their lovemaking took on a volatility that resembled a long sequence of exploding dynamite charges. Noah ravaged her senses and her mouth as their bodies slammed together, their journey a wild ride into heaven and hell. Heaven because the feelings were so rich and encompassing, hell because he feared that there might be an end to them.

Maggie peaked unexpectedly, a stunned cry escaping her as she shattered inside. He felt the inner shudders that milked his flesh and nearly pushed him over the edge. He longed to follow her into oblivion, but he resisted the temptation her climax posed. Gathering her against his chest, Noah ceased all movement until her breathing steadied and she regained her awareness of him several minutes later.

"You surprised me," Maggie whispered as she curved her hand against the side of his face. "How did you manage to get inside?"

He smiled, the sensual nature of his thoughts obvious as he pondered his reply. He arched a dark brow, the expression on his face wholly arrogant and thoroughly male as he framed her face between his hands and peered down at her.

She laughed softly. "You know what I mean."

Her humor tremored low in her body. He felt the corresponding tugging sensations deep in his loins. He sucked air into his burning lungs, then settled more forcefully against her.

"Answer me," she insisted breathlessly.

"The key you hide under the flowerpot on the back steps."

He dipped his head and dropped a hard kiss on her lips. She shifted both hands to the back of his neck, holding him still as she laved the width of his lower lip, then darted her tongue into the hot recesses of his mouth.

His maleness, still lodged within her, clenched. Noah shuddered, then sucked at her teasing tongue before catching the tip between his teeth. He began to move inside her again, slowly, torturously plumbing her depths. Her fingers flexed against his shoulders, digging into his skin. He deliberately escalated the length and pace of his thrusts, taking immense satisfaction in her breathy sighs and from the shudders that rippled through her.

Maggie's hips moved in counterpoint to his as a cascade of erotic sensations shivered through every centimeter of her body. She murmured inarticulate words into his mouth as she angled her head and deepened their kiss even more. She felt the totality of Noah's possession, and she gloried in the feeling.

Doubt nibbled at the edge of her happiness, though, forcing her to push aside, if only for the time being, the nagging awareness that she tempted fate by even being in Noah's arms. She needed this one last night with him, needed the memories they were making, not just the incredible sense of being and feeling completely alive for the first time in her life.

His force increased. Her body quaked and quivered beneath his. She lied to herself in the moments that followed, lied as he etched himself into her sensory memory by telling herself that her recollection of their time together would comfort her once she ended their affair.

Her thoughts scattered, her sense of reality disappearing in the minutes that followed. Swept away on currents of desire-saturated sensation, Maggie completely surrendered to the driving force of Noah's consuming passion.

Reaching between their bodies, he touched the pearl of sensitive nerve endings already aroused by their joining. She cried out, her reaction to his intimate stroking instantaneous, explosive. He drove into her again and again, not allowing her to come down from the summit she'd scaled. She grew wild beneath him, bucking against him as her highly stimulated body succumbed to yet another mind-numbing climax.

"I can't stop," he said in a raw, hunger-filled voice.

"Don't," she whimpered, clinging tightly to him because he seemed to be the only stable force in her universe. "Don't ever stop, Noah."

He didn't. He couldn't. He felt alive when he was inside her. Intimacy held his worry at bay, even permitted him the luxury of believing that anything was possible. Not believing would have killed him.

He rolled free of her, soothing her cry of alarm with reassuring words as he turned her onto her stomach, moved behind her, and lifted her hips. He eased into her, one hand stroking her from hips to nape, the other fitted over her pelvis. He tantalized her with his fingertips.

He surged into her, his hands and fingers playing over her body with the skill of a concert musician. She sheathed him even more tightly than before, wringing a primal sound of pleasure from Noah. The minutes that followed were filled with the intensity of a man dedicated to a quest that would determine his destiny. He took Maggie with him, loving her with his body. He felt her answering passion as she met each invasive thrust and heard it in the wild sounds that slipped past her lips.

She rocked backward, stiffened suddenly as her insides started to fly apart, and then felt herself being hurled directly into another release. Intense beyond belief, it consumed her in a blaze of incendiary sensation. "I love you," she moaned as she gave herself up to the intense feelings devastating her mind and body.

Noah's rigid control snapped, his ability to contain himself compromised by three simple words. He forgot about control, forgot about everything but Maggie and the agonizing ecstasy streaking through him like a blazing comet.

He called out her name, the hoarse sound dragged from his depths as he climaxed. He filled her with his love and the hot force of his turbulent passion, the sustained quality of his release bunching the muscles of his body to the point of pain.

Several minutes later he carefully eased out of

her before he collapsed across the bed at her side. She turned into him, holding him close to her heart. Her lips whispered across his chest, and she murmured words that the deafening roar of his heartbeat kept him from hearing.

Noah closed his eyes, his breathing still ragged. He reminded himself not to drift off, reminded himself that he and Maggie had things to resolve, but his body had other ideas thanks to the manner in which he'd driven himself during the negotiations.

Maggie exhaled shallowly, not wanting to disturb Noah as he relaxed and fell asleep. She understood his fatigue. He'd pushed himself almost ruthlessly during the preceding seventy-two hours, and she now suspected that he hadn't rested at all between sessions at the estate. Although grateful for the chance to watch over him while he slept, her own exhaustion eventually claimed her and she dozed off shortly before dawn.

Noah awoke with a start, Maggie's arms still wrapped around him, her cheek pressed against his chest. He glanced at the window, taking in the blazing summer sun that had already announced the arrival of a new day.

"Good morning," she said quietly.

He peered down at her in the same instant that she looked up. He saw her smile, but uneasiness leapt to life inside him when he noticed the sadness that tinged her facial expression. His heart went utterly still in his chest for a very long moment. He knew then what she intended. He winced, but he kept his gaze steady.

"We need to talk, Noah."

"I agree." He reluctantly separated their bodies. Swinging his legs to the side of the bed, Noah paused to massage the back of his neck. Not willing to be rushed, he took a moment to think.

Maggie was right, he silently conceded. They did need to talk, but he didn't intend to conduct a conversation with her while they were both naked, before he drank at least one cup of strong black coffee, or until he pulled his emotions and thoughts into some semblance of order. The rest of his life was at stake, and he was done playing games.

Pushing to his feet, Noah walked naked into the bathroom, his thoughts still faintly muddled by fatigue as he turned on the shower and stepped under the sharp spray. It began to anger him as he washed that he felt none of the emotional certainty of a man who was loved. Frustrated by that realization and a few others concerning Maggie Holden, he showered quickly, dried off, located his trousers, and followed the scent of freshly brewed coffee into the empty kitchen.

After pouring himself a cup, Noah paused at the kitchen sink and peered out the window. Maggie stood in the middle of her rose garden, clad in a white silk caftan and matching slippers. Tears streamed down her cheeks.

The sight of her in such emotional pain almost

broke his heart, but he refused to go to her, refused to tell her that it would be okay if she ran from the love they felt for each other.

This time, Noah realized, he wanted her to come to him. This time, he expected her to trust his love and be guided by her own instincts.

ELEVEN

"Would you like some breakfast?" Maggie asked after walking back into the cottage and making her way to the kitchen. Determined to maintain her poise, she attempted a smile as she looked at Noah.

"No." He spoke sharply as he finished filling his coffee mug for the second time. Turning to face her, he simply looked at her, his facial features set in unforgiving lines and hard angles.

Stricken but not surprised by his anger, Maggie's smile turned into a grimace. She drew in a steadying breath and brought her hands together in front of her body. Noah's gaze flicked to her joined palms, his jaw tightening, then back to her face.

She let her hands fall to her sides, painfully aware of the transparency of her body language where he was concerned. She waited for him to end the silence between them, but his expression remained remote.

She tried again, wanting to ease the tension between them even though she sensed the futility of her efforts before she spoke. "It's really no trouble if you're hungry."

He muttered a distinctly obscene word, turned on his heel, and left the room.

Maggie felt as though she'd just been slapped. She reminded herself that Noah understood her far better than anyone she'd ever known, and that she shouldn't be surprised by his obvious frustration with her. She also recognized his inclination to become intractable when he was angry, but she knew he wouldn't turn her into a target. That had been Randall's inclination, but never Noah's.

She followed him to the sunporch. Drawing on what remained of her waning courage, Maggie made herself say the words she'd been practicing in the rose garden for the last fifteen minutes. "Regardless of what we feel for each other, what happened between us last night can't happen again."

Noah behaved as though she hadn't even spoken. He settled into a chair and stretched his long legs out in front of him. He took a drink of coffee, then another, his gaze level as he consumed most of the contents of the mug.

"Did you hear me?" she asked, unnerved by his silent perusal.

"Sit down, Maggie."

His hard voice made her flinch.

"Sit down," he ordered, his anger no longer concealed behind a glacial expression. His hazel eyes were almost black with fury, even though his leanly muscled body looked remarkably relaxed.

"Don't speak to me in that tone of voice," she flared defensively.

"Then sit down," he said so softly that she had to strain to hear him.

She remained standing. "I meant what I said. We can't be together again, Noah. There's no point in pursuing a relationship that can't last."

"You love me," he said.

She felt as though he'd stabbed her with an invisible blade. "You misunderstood me last night." She barely got the words past her lips.

"Don't lie to me or to yourself."

Maggie's legs suddenly gave out, and she sank onto the love seat positioned across from his chair. A low coffee table separated them physically, but the gulf she felt on an emotional level was several miles wide.

"I'm not . . ." She stopped, feeling stupid. She couldn't deny that she loved him. Somehow, she knew, she had to persuade him that her desire to end their relationship was based on her love for him, and nothing else. "All right, I lied. I do love you, Noah. I've fallen in love with you, but I won't have an affair with you."

"I don't recall suggesting one."

She flushed. "You know what I mean."

"No, I don't know what you mean. Spell it out for me, why don't you? Make some sense out of what you're feeling right now, for both our sakes," he suggested, sounding again like the internationally lauded mediator who'd just orchestrated a political compromise that lesser men had tried and failed to accomplish in recent years.

She dropped her gaze to her lap, staring at her tangled fingers. Pretending not to be upset was useless, so she ceased trying. "When you first showed up on my front porch, I was terrified of you. I almost got into my car and drove away after accepting your dinner invitation," she confessed. "I realized that anyone who knew about our working relationship had to know that we were good friends a long time ago, and I was convinced that State had sent you to dig around in my past. I honestly thought they were using you to get to me, which is why I was so paranoid at first. I was wrong, but it took me a while before I really believed that you weren't here for any reasons other than your own."

She trembled. Darting a glance at Noah, she saw that he'd set aside his coffee mug and that his fists were clenched on his thighs. "Are you listening to me?"

"Keep talking," he urged quietly.

"You helped me learn how to trust again, Noah," she said with quiet dignity. "Thanks to you, I started feeling my emotions, I rediscovered my optimism, and I reclaimed my confidence, both personally and professionally." Maggie smiled sadly. "You've supported and encouraged me in ways that still amaze me. You seduced me back into the world."

"Temporarily, it seems," he remarked.

Maggie shook her head. "No. Permanently. I can't even begin to express my gratitude that you—"

"Screw gratitude!"

"—cared enough about me to make the effort," she said in spite of his interruption. "I'll be in your debt for the rest of my life, but I still can't have a relationship with you. It wouldn't be wise for either one of us. We want different things."

He slammed his empty mug on the coffee table and began to clap his hands. "Great farewell speech."

"Noah, you're not being fair!"

"And I never will be where you're concerned, so you damn well better adjust to that reality."

"Why?" she whispered.

"I want you."

"You've had me," she bluntly pointed out. Her memories of the intimacy she'd experienced with him still shook her to her core. She knew she would never experience anything like it again, and the impending loss already hurt. "There are other women. Women far better suited . . ."

"I don't want other women."

"I'm not available."

Noah surged to his feet and made his way to

the glass wall that overlooked the rose garden. After a moment, he turned to look at her. "You're a lousy candidate for spinsterhood. There's too much fire in you."

"Only with you," she said in a subdued voice.

"Then why cut and run?"

"I'm not. I'm doing what's necessary."

"What about children?"

She paled. He knew she wanted a family. In her heart, she knew she wanted it with him.

"Please don't," she managed, choking on the emotion that closed her throat.

He ignored her plea. "You can marry a man you don't love and endure a marriage you'll hate, you can adopt, or you can try artificial insemination."

She angrily got to her feet. Noah approached her, blocking her attempt to distance herself from him and his remarks.

"I won't listen to this."

He grabbed her arm. "You'll listen, because I'm fighting for my life. Besides, you owe us, Maggie."

"This is a crazy conversation."

"I want you. I've gone too many years without you."

"You have other options," she insisted through gritted teeth. The thought of Noah making love to another woman made her feel physically ill, but she forged ahead. "Any woman would be glad to—"

"Not interested. Try another tactic, because you just lost a lot of points on that one."

Exhaling shakily, she pulled free of Noah's grasp, then brought her fingertips to her temples. Her head throbbed. "This isn't a debate. Our affair is over, so you should leave now."

"I'm not going anywhere. We're not finished talking."

"Noah!" she exclaimed, so rattled that she spoke without thinking. "I love you too much to ever risk hurting you. It would kill me to be responsible for destroying your career. I refuse to do it."

His gaze narrowed. She saw a look of satisfaction in his hard-featured face.

"Finally," he muttered. "You have finally gotten to the heart of this idiotic but very noble decision of yours, haven't you?"

"Quit with the insults," she ordered, angered by his remark. "I'm trying to protect you."

"Just love me. The rest can be dealt with."

"No," she said stubbornly. "You cannot have a woman with my past in your life. It's crazy to believe that you can. You'd jeopardize everything you've worked to build during the last twenty years, and then you'd wind up hating me. I couldn't stand it if that happened."

"You're wrong. I thought I'd proven that to you during the last few days. You had the highest security level clearance issued by State."

"*You* secured the clearance. They wouldn't have given me one on my own."

He walked to the telephone. Picking up the receiver, he punched out several numbers. He didn't bother with the amenities, simply barked, "Peterson, explain Ms. Holden's clearance status to her."

Stunned, she accepted the telephone when Noah handed it to her, listening numbly as she was told that her clearance requests wouldn't be denied in the future. She handed the receiver back to Noah, who dropped it into the phone's cradle.

"Satisfied?" he asked.

"That's only one hurdle," she reminded him. "People remember me, even though I use my maiden name now."

"People like Rostov? Wake up, Maggie. Rostov's a lackey in the diplomatic community. He can't hurt you. Do I need to remind you that you, not me or anyone else, effectively neutralized him?"

"Other delegates remembered me," she persisted. "Three different people made a point of telling me that they knew my identity, even though I'd changed my name. Noah, they remembered Randall Hartley's widow, the woman rumored to have committed treason against her own country."

"We both know that was a lie."

"It doesn't matter. There are enough people out there who think I'm guilty. State certainly still believes it, even though you strong-armed them into giving me a clearance. You know as well as I do that they wouldn't approve a clearance for me if I went to them on my own. The rumors alone that will fly through Washington about my integrity could harm your reputation, and I won't permit that to happen a second time. You deserve far better."

"You are so damnably stubborn," he said, then switched gears. "The president sends his regards."

She stared at him, genuinely off balance by his comment. "What?"

"You heard me. The president remembers you from the summits we worked on with him during his UN days. He liked you."

Peterson at State was one thing, but the president? Maggie took a shallow breath. "I don't know what to say."

He looked genuinely amused then. "Well, you'd better think of something to say to the man, and to the First Lady, because we're invited to a private family dinner at the White House next week."

"He invited you," she corrected.

"*Us*. I told him we're a team again. I've waited too long, Maggie. I will not wait any longer. I can't."

Confusion reigned inside her. "You make it sound as though . . ." She couldn't say the words. They were trapped in her throat, wedged there by disbelief and shock.

"As though I've always loved you?" he said quietly as he curved his broad-palmed hands over her shoulders.

She still couldn't speak, so she hesitantly nodded.

"I have."

Her chin trembled. Tears flooded her eyes. "Why did you keep silent?"

"When I realized my feelings, it was too late. You were only a few weeks from your wedding day when I figured out what I was about to lose. You seemed happy."

"I was in those days."

He nodded as he peered down at her. "Don't cry. There's no need."

There was every need, she thought as she glimpsed the anguish and loneliness he'd endured in his dark eyes. "Noah," she choked out, her tears spilling free. "I never suspected."

"Of course you didn't. I made sure of it. I didn't want to put you in an awkward position. I sure as hell didn't want to see pity in your eyes when you looked at me."

"But you walked me down the aisle on my wedding day."

He drew her into his heat and strength and held her. "That was the toughest day of my life. It almost killed me, but it was what you wanted."

"Dear heaven, I'm so sorry."

"Don't be. I created my own hell. I want it

over with, though. You're the only one who can end it."

She hugged him, desperately wanting to believe that he was right.

"I want you as a full partner in my life," he continued on. "I want your love, your laughter, your ability to make a real home, your kindness to people who are upset or vulnerable, and your linguistic talent. I want all of you. I trust you. You understand me, and you accept me as I am. I've never found your equal anywhere, and I spent a lot of energy looking. I love you and need you, Maggie. If you're honest with yourself, you'll see that we need each other. We can make it work, if you'll give us a chance."

"You have so much faith in me," she whispered, swayed by his honesty and the stunning totality of his love.

"I always have, so that's not about to change."

He leaned down then, took her face between his hands, and kissed her. He lingered at her lips, the epitome of a man with all the time in the world at his disposal as he explored the taste and textures he found there. His tongue dipped inside when she parted her lips and angled her head. She tasted the heady flavors of his passion.

Maggie felt her heart race and her senses spin wildly out of control. When Noah released her lips, she frowned suddenly, a line from a book she'd once read popping into her head. "You want me in the bedroom and the boardroom, which is why you've been conducting this one-man campaign to resurrect my self-esteem." She shook her head in amazement. "You and your multiple agendas."

He shrugged, and didn't look the least bit guilty. "You resurrected your own self-esteem. I just gave you a nudge. And for the record, my needs where you're concerned extend far beyond the boundaries of the bedroom and the boardroom. You're my best friend. You're the woman I love. And, God willing, you'll be the mother of my children. I will always love you and need you, Maggie-mine, and I'll never know any real happiness if I don't have you in every aspect of my life. That happens to include my consulting operation, because I need you with me there, as well."

She looked up at him, her eyes shining with love and hope. Noah was the kind of man who would stand loyally at her side no matter what happened. Adversity challenged him, made him relentless in his efforts to defend those who couldn't defend themselves, while love seemed to enhance his inner strength.

She sensed that when tough times came, which she knew they would, they would face them as true partners. Because she'd had a sampling of that partnership during the previous month and a half, Maggie craved the life he offered almost as much as she craved daily doses of his love and passion.

She realized then that she wanted Noah enough to take the risks that he'd already willingly embraced on her behalf. Letting gossip and innuendo deprive her of happiness with Noah or dictate her future suddenly seemed the poorest of judgments. She couldn't imagine a life without him any longer. Maggie didn't want to imagine her life without him.

"I love you, Noah. Oh God, I love you so much."

He held her, emotion too overwhelming to articulate filling his eyes. He pressed a kiss to the top of Maggie's head, then tightened his embrace. A shudder ripped through him moments later, and she looked up at him.

"Ask me," she urged softly.

"Will you marry me?"

She smiled. "Yes! A thousand times yes!"

"Tell me why you've finally changed your mind."

She lifted up on tiptoe and kissed him. He devoured her mouth, and they were both shaking with desire when they drew apart.

"Tell me why, Maggie-mine."

"I meant it when I said you'd seduced me back into the world. The simple truth is that my life won't ever be complete unless you're a part of it."

He smiled. "Speaking of being seduced . . ."

She wrapped her arms around his neck once he'd lifted her up and cradled her against his chest. "Do we have to talk about it?"

"Absolutely not. This is one of those times when actions speak louder than words."

Their mingling laughter trailed behind them as Noah carried her through the house to her bedroom. He thoroughly seduced her. She returned the favor in kind.

THE EDITORS' CORNER

If it's love you're looking for, you've come to the right place. Our TREASURED TALES IV romances brim with excitement and adventure as your favorite authors add a sexy contemporary spin to everyone's favorite classics. Each of these wonderful novels features memorable characters finding love in the unlikeliest of places. TREASURED TALES IV is your invitation to join them on the most romantic journey of all.

Goldilocks is more than a match for three big, bad bears in Debra Dixon's **BAD TO THE BONE**, LOVESWEPT #774. He's a brand of danger she's never risked, with the most unforgiving pair of blue eyes that ever stared into her troubled soul, yet Jessica Daniels insists she doesn't have the answers to Detective Sullivan Kincaid's questions about a missing person. But the innocent act doesn't fit with the way the mysterious brunette arouses Sully's suspicions—and his most forbidden desires. Debra Dixon delivers a once-in-a-lifetime read with this powerfully emotional, savagely sensual, yet utterly romantic novel.

Romance Writers of America president Janis Reams Hudson delights with **ANGEL ON A HARLEY**, LOVESWEPT #775. Just as Whitney Houston confounds Kevin Costner in the instant classic movie THE BODYGUARD, Faith Hillman isn't at all what Dalton McShane expects when he faces the woman who claims she is carrying his child. And Dalton McShane isn't what she's been expecting either. Right name, wrong guy . . . Clearly, Faith is a woman betrayed—big time. Then, an act of violence makes it obvious that if ever there is a woman in need of a knight in shining armor, Faith is it. Weaving a story of forbidden passion and potent seduction, of unspoken dreams and second chances, Janis Reams Hudson celebrates the sweet power of enduring love and its healing magic.

MIDNIGHT HEAT, LOVESWEPT #776, is the provocative finale to Donna Kauffman's THE THREE MUSKETEERS trilogy. They call him The Predator, the investigator who never leaves a case unsolved, and now Dane Colbourne has set his sights on her! Adria Burke knows her quick response prevented a tragic midair collision, but Dane wants evidence that proves her case—and his fierce, hot look tells her he wants her just as much. When men who'll risk anything finally taste irresistible danger in the arms of women who can't help getting a little too close to the flame, there's no one better to write their stories than Donna Kauffman.

Last but by no means least, Faye Hughes shines

with star power in **WILD AT HEART**, LOVESWEPT #777, inspired by the timelessly appealing movie IT HAPPENED ONE NIGHT. In Faye's delicious homage, Jake Wilder crashes a party looking for scandal and maybe a chance at redemption, but when Maggie Thorpe drags him into a closet to elude his pursuers, what else could he do but kiss her breathless? Her untamed heart recognizes a kindred spirit beneath Jake's outrageous charm, but once they team up to expose a shady deal, the sinfully sexy reporter must convince the rebel heiress they are meant to be partners in passion forever. Sparkling with wicked fun and seductive as a Southern drawl from a bad boy's lips, this tantalizing tale of love in close quarters shows just why Faye Hughes is a fan favorite every time!

Happy reading!

With warmest wishes,

Beth de Guzman
Senior Editor

Shauna Summers
Associate Editor

P.S. Watch for these Bantam women's fiction titles coming in February: *New York Times* bestselling author Iris Johansen weaves her special brand of magic with **LION'S BRIDE,** a sizzling new novel of passion, danger, and sensuality. **SEE HOW THEY RUN** is a gripping novel of romantic suspense in the tradition of Joy Fielding by acclaimed talent Bethany Campbell, and Elizabeth Elliott follows up her spectacular Fanfare debut of THE WARLORD with **SCOUNDREL**—a story of passion in a world of war and intrigue where the greatest danger of all is in daring to love. Be sure to see next month's LOVESWEPTs for a preview of these exceptional novels. And immediately following this page, preview the Bantam women's fiction titles on sale *now!*

Don't miss these extraordinary books
by your favorite Bantam authors

On sale in December:

BREAKFAST IN BED

by Sandra Brown

NIGHT SINS

by Tami Hoag

VANITY

by Jane Feather

DEATH ELIGIBLE

by Judith Henry Wall

SAXON BRIDE

by Tamara Leigh

Her novels are sensual and moving, compelling and richly satisfying. That's why Sandra Brown is one of America's best-loved romance writers. Now, the New York Times *bestselling author of* HEAVEN'S PRICE *captures the wrenching dilemma of a woman tempted by an unexpected —and forbidden—love.*

BREAKFAST IN BED

by Sandra Brown

"No one understands sexual fantasy better than Sandra Brown. . . . Ms. Brown inventively blends a variety of fantasies into the fabric of her very real romance."

—*Romantic Times*

Erotic, touching, and true, BREAKFAST IN BED *is one of Sandra Brown's classic romances available in hardcover for the first time.*

NOW AVAILABLE IN PAPERBACK

NIGHT SINS

The terrifying national bestseller by

Tami Hoag

"Lock the doors and windows and turn on all the lights—a spine-chilling thriller."
—*New Woman*

"NIGHT SINS starts fast and doesn't let up until the chilling climax. Tami Hoag has written a winner."
—Phillip Margolin

"Tami Hoag writes the kind of can't-put-it-down suspense that keeps you on the edge to the final sentence."
—John Saul

From the nationally bestselling author of
VALENTINE and VIOLET

VANITY

by Jane Feather

From romance's newest rising star comes a new triumph of romance. Brimming with passionate emotion and compelling adventure, here is Jane Feather at her most unforgettable.

"I presume you too have a name, sir," she said in an attempt to recapture her earlier assurance.

"Oh, most certainly," he agreed, taking a japanned snuffbox from the deep pocket of his coat. He flicked the lid and delicately took a pinch.

Nothing else was forthcoming. Octavia tapped her foot on the stone lintel. "Am I to be told it, sir?"

He looked at her, one eyebrow quizzically raised. "I confess I hadn't given the question any thought. However . . ." He bowed, managing an elegant flourish in the confined space. "At this moment Lord Nick is at your service, Miss Morgan."

She stared at him, trying to remember where she'd heard the name before. And what did he mean by *at this moment*? "Oh?" she said, her jaw dropping. "Lord Nick, the highwayman?"

He smiled and shrugged. "Such calumny. I don't know where people get these stories from."

Octavia shook her head as if trying to clear her thoughts. No gentleman, after all, but Lord Nick, the highwayman given the devil's colloquial name for his uncanny ability to evade the law. If he was who he said he was—not that he looked in the least as she'd imagined a highwayman would look—then it seemed unlikely he was intending to lay a charge against her. But it seemed only reasonable and friendly in the circumstances to return his property without further delay. She slipped her hand inside her cloak, sliding her fingers into the slit in her gown, intending to extract the watch from the pouch. Then she realized that he was watching her every movement, a sardonic spark in his eyes.

She let her hand fall to her side and smiled nonchalantly. She didn't like the look in those slate-gray eyes, and this was far too public a spot for an unsolicited admission of guilt, even to a fellow pirate.

The rushing mob was diminishing now, the cries and screams fading into the distance.

"Come," Lord Nick said. "I think it's safe to leave now."

"You go your way and I'll go mine, sir," she said, stepping out of the doorway. There was no sign now of a sedan chair; the chairmen would have made off to safety as soon as the cry of "press gang" had gone up —they were strong, well-muscled men, perfect candidates for His Majesty's Navy.

"You seem remarkably obtuse for someone who I'm convinced has a sharp head on her shoulders," her companion remarked in a tone of mild exasperation. "We have yet to have our little discussion, if you recall." He looked round, getting his bearings. "My horse is at the Rose and Crown . . . this way, I believe."

"I'm not coming with you," Octavia said quietly, her anger visible only in her snapping eyes and her increased pallor. "I don't know what you have in mind, but if you attempt to abduct me, I'll scream so loudly it'll bring every constable in the area."

He appeared not to have heard her, his attention directed toward the lad bringing his horse, a big-shouldered roan who looked easily capable of carrying two riders.

"Now, Miss Morgan . . . pillion or in front of me?" He turned back to her. "Either will be perfectly comfortable, I assure you. Peter is as steady as a rock."

"Are you perhaps hard of hearing?" Octavia asked, her voice low and fierce. "I bid you good day." She spun on her heel and stalked out of the yard, her back prickling as she waited for the arresting hand on her shoulder. But nothing happened. She walked unmolested out of the yard of the Rose and Crown and into the narrow cobbled lane.

The pounding of hooves behind her at first didn't intrude on her reverie. When they did, they were almost upon her. She was hurrying down the center of the lane, avoiding the filthy water and refuse in the kennel at the side. Now she had no choice but to jump sideways, splashing through the kennel, if she wasn't to be run down. It was a common enough hazard in the side streets of the city.

"A pox on your knavish soul!" she swore in most unladylike accents as the kennel filth caked her boots and soiled the hem of her cloak and gown that she hadn't had time to lift clear. "May you rot in . . ."

The rest of the curse was lost as the rider drew

abreast of her, swooped low in the saddle, and caught her up with all the dexterity of a performer at Philip Astley's Amphitheatre.

Octavia found herself in the saddle of the roan, the hard body of Lord Nick at her back, his encircling arm holding her steady on her perch.

She opened her mouth and screamed, a shrill, piercing clamor. Casements were flung open along the lane, curious faces hanging out, peering down through the thickening veil of snow.

"You wish to visit the local magistrate?" Lord Nick murmured against her ear, making no attempt to still her screams. "I'm sure he'll be interested in what you're concealing beneath your skirt."

"Let me down and I'll give you back your goddamned watch!" Octavia exclaimed.

"Oh, yes, you will give it back to me," he agreed equably. "All in good time, though, Miss Morgan. All in good time."

DEATH ELIGIBLE

by the bestselling author of
MOTHER LOVE

Judith Henry Wall

A family is held together by bonds stronger than the law. But what happens when that family must make a choice to give up one of its own? Could they sacrifice their own mentally handicapped son to save the life of one of his siblings? In this mesmerizing new novel, Judith Henry Wall asks this provocative question as she plumbs the depths of one family's secret heart.

The police had come just as they were sitting down to dinner—to arrest him for murder. Hours later, Maura cleared away the uneaten meal, stopping every few minutes to wipe her eyes with her apron.

Angie took a sip of water to help the cracker go down and took another from the package.

Had the rest of the household been able to sleep, she wondered, or had they, like her, in spite of bourbon and sleeping pills, replayed the horrible scenario of Danny's being arrested over and over? And the ten o'clock news. Danny being dragged into the city jail.

She'd been sitting here at this same table on the morning of her twenty-first birthday, when her parents asked if they could name her Danny's guardian in their wills—darling Danny, who was even then taller than Angie but would remain forever a child.

Angie was surprised that her parents felt the need

to ask. She'd always assumed that she eventually would be the family member to assume responsibility for Danny. But assumptions weren't enough for her parents. They needed a formal commitment from her. They wanted her to look them in the eye and say yes, she would be Danny's guardian after they were gone.

Angie had come around the table to kneel between her parents, to put her arms around them and say, of course, she would look after Danny. Always.

She accepted responsibility for him even though being his guardian would limit her options and complicate her life. But she loved him too much not to. Her love for him was unconditional. Even maternal.

Angie pushed the package of crackers away and took another sip of water. All about her, the house was heavy with silence.

She'd told the arresting officers not to handcuff Danny. He couldn't stand to be restrained. And he was so strong. He used a shoulder to slam one officer against the wall and his head to knock the other one off his feet. One of them had actually reached for his handgun when her father's voice suddenly resounded through the entry hall. "Get out of here—both of you. I'll take my son to jail myself."

"I'm sorry, Judge Tarrington, but you know we can't do that," the older detective explained.

"The hell you can't," he'd said, pointing to the door. "I will call the mayor, the police commissioner, the governor, the president, and God himself if you don't take off those damned handcuffs and get out of here!"

But Danny would have it all to go through again

Monday morning when they handcuffed him and dragged him into a courtroom, where he'd be asked how he pled—guilty or not guilty of killing Beth Williams.

Angie tried to think—did Danny even know what the word "guilty" meant?

"Oh, God," she said out loud.

At first, after he didn't die of the encephalitis that left him mentally impaired, he'd been a happy little soul, unless he thought someone was mad at him. Then he would cry. Even when he was a pest, they were seldom mean to him. Except Matt. Matt had little patience with his retarded twin.

But after the kidnaping, Danny came home a changed boy. He screamed if startled. His feelings were easily hurt. He had nightmares. He got hysterical if restrained. A mama cat got upset with his handling of her babies and scratched his hand. Danny stomped on the cat and killed it. And he beat up Manuel's son after he jumped out from behind a bush and said "boo"—really beat him, breaking his nose and collarbone.

Beth came to live in the room next to Danny's after the kidnaping—after it was decided to keep Danny at home, where he would be safe, where no strange woman would walk onto the school playground and take him away.

When Beth first came to them, she was twenty years old, a special-education major at UT-Arlington. Frank had been eighteen, Angie fifteen, Julia twelve, Danny and Matt almost eight. Their parents had called everyone into the living room to meet her. Beth, wearing a crisp white blouse and a navy skirt, was standing in front of the high arched window, her mass of hair a halo of golden red in the sunlight.

After Beth came, Danny did better, even started singing again. Beth taught Danny to count and write his name. She taught him to swim and when it was all right to laugh and sing and when he was supposed to be a very quiet boy. She encouraged him to run sprints, timing him, training him, teaching him technique. When he was the first runner across the finish line in the 100-yard-dash finals of the 1980 Special Olympics, the whole family cheered and wept with the joy of it. It was a miracle. And they had Beth to thank for it.

But Danny never completely lost the dark side that he brought home from the kidnaping. His nightmares became occasional, but when he had them, they were terrible. And what had previously manifested itself as frustration when he couldn't work a puzzle or color inside the lines would sometimes cause him to dissolve into bouts of uncontrollable crying. The whole family learned to intercede when tears threatened, to redirect his attention to some other activity. It hurt too much to see Danny cry. Sometimes all that was required was to hug him, even after he was no longer a little boy, even when physically he was the largest member of the family, larger even than his twin brother. Danny needed lots of hugs. Because of him, they were a family of huggers.

Looking back, Angie often wondered if the kidnapers hadn't meant to take Matt, the normal twin. Those outside the family always seemed to regard Danny as some sort of stepchild or charity case and not a true Tarrington.

But Danny made them special and defined them as a family. He taught them tolerance and patience. He shared his wonder at the world with them—and his innocence, even after he was grown, with whiskers on his chin and a disturbing fascination for anything female.

Beth didn't have a family. Angie couldn't imagine such a thing. With three brothers and a sister, she had always been surrounded by family. Her Tarrington grandparents lived behind them, just the other side of the back gate. And her family visited frequently with her mother's parents, who had retired in Austin.

Angie and her little sister, Julia, decided right away that Beth was to be part of their family. Their big sister. And it did seem that way sometimes. But they were born Tarringtons, and Beth only worked for their family. She wanted it, though—to be a Tarrington. None of them realized how much.

SAXON BRIDE

by the author of
PAGAN BRIDE

Tamara Leigh

Once Maxen Pendery was a man of God. Then he was told that his brother had been murdered by a Saxon wench, and he knew he could not rest until he took revenge. Yet when he finally captured Rhiannyn of Etheverry, something unexpected stirred within him. True, she was breathtakingly lovely; but never once did she use her woman's wiles to battle him, only her sharp tongue and strong will . . . leaving Maxen torn between his duty and an agonizing truth: he would do anything to conquer this golden-haired maid, even if the price was his very soul.

Maxen, now Brother Justus to the Saxons, watched Rhiannyn cross the glade behind Edwin. At first sight he had been uncertain she was the same woman who had spent so many weeks in the castle dungeons, for her resemblance to that creature was distant.

But it was she, and even more lovely than he'd imagined she would be beneath the dirt, grime, and bruises. Hair that had only whispered of gold now gleamed that color, the cream of her skin was accented by the tint of roses in each cheek, and a shape that had promised much beneath her tattered bliaut had more than fulfilled its promise in the belted tunic and hose she wore to practice her swordskill. She was beautiful, almost angelic, and more than capable of luring spellbound men to their death.

Aye, it was Rhiannyn of Etheverry, though stronger than before. Maxen had felt her resolve, seen it in her eyes, her carriage, and her stiffening back when Edwin had called her to task. A small woman with the strength of many.

But he would break her, Maxen vowed, his resentment over the hold she had on him lending him determination. Then the woman who was a scourge to the vows of his body—vows she had forced him to renounce—would be forever exorcised.

As the man called Aethel came toward him, Maxen glanced one last time at Rhiannyn. Positioned before the pel, she assumed the proper stance and angled her sword in readiness for a mock attack. Though she did not look to Edwin, he spoke to her, gestured, then stepped back.

As Maxen had wondered whether Thomas had lain with Rhiannyn, he now wondered the same about Edwin, but then Rhiannyn dealt the wooden post an admirable blow and sped his thoughts elsewhere. He frowned. Perhaps she had spoken true, he reflected. Mayhap it was she who had murdered Thomas after all. Though he thought it, he still was not convinced. It had to be another.

With that in mind, Maxen swept his searching gaze over those who had returned to their intense training and, surprisingly, found that many appeared quite worthy. Their swings strong, their aim sure, they promised a well-matched battle when next they set themselves upon the castle to take back what they claimed was theirs. And it was theirs, a vexatious voice reminded him.

Had been theirs, he countered, but no more. Regardless, he must not forget his reason for coming into Edwin's grim world.

Though Maxen had experienced doubt when he'd listened in on Rhiannyn's conversation with Christophe and heard her tell him that it was not Edwin who had killed Thomas, he had only believed it after following her to this place and seeing the injury to the man's fighting arm. As Rhiannyn had said, it would have been impossible for him to have thrown the dagger after receiving such a serious wound. Assuredly, it had not been Edwin; but who then? Which one of these men had plunged his dagger into Thomas's heart and bled his life upon that field?

A fire growing in him, Maxen lowered his gaze so the great, hulking Aethel would not see the betraying depths of his eyes.

Aye, he told himself in an attempt to calm his blood, soon every last one of Edwin's rebels would know the yoke of Norman rule, including Rhiannyn. First, though, he must discover who had murdered Thomas and insure that the villain did not simply die but that he suffered as Thomas had.

On sale in January:

LION'S BRIDE
by Iris Johansen

SEE HOW THEY RUN
by Bethany Campbell

SCOUNDREL
by Elizabeth Elliott

To enter the sweepstakes outlined below, you must respond by the date specified and follow all entry instructions published elsewhere in this offer.

DREAM COME TRUE SWEEPSTAKES

Sweepstakes begins 9/1/94, ends 1/15/96. To qualify for the Early Bird Prize, entry must be received by the date specified elsewhere in this offer. Winners will be selected in random drawings on 2/29/96 by an independent judging organization whose decisions are final. Early Bird winner will be selected in a separate drawing from among all qualifying entries.

Odds of winning determined by total number of entries received. Distribution not to exceed 300 million.

Estimated maximum retail value of prizes: Grand (1) $25,000 (cash alternative $20,000); First (1) $2,000; Second (1) $750; Third (50) $75; Fourth (1,000) $50; Early Bird (1) $5,000. Total prize value: $86,500.

Automobile and travel trailer must be picked up at a local dealer; all other merchandise prizes will be shipped to winners. Awarding of any prize to a minor will require written permission of parent/guardian. If a trip prize is won by a minor, s/he must be accompanied by parent/legal guardian. Trip prizes subject to availability and must be completed within 12 months of date awarded. Blackout dates may apply. Early Bird trip is on a space available basis and does not include port charges, gratuities, optional shore excursions and onboard personal purchases. Prizes are not transferable or redeemable for cash except as specified. No substitution for prizes except as necessary due to unavailability. Travel trailer and/or automobile license and registration fees are winners' responsibility as are any other incidental expenses not specified herein.

Early Bird Prize may not be offered in some presentations of this sweepstakes. Grand through third prize winners will have the option of selecting any prize offered at level won. All prizes will be awarded. Drawing will be held at 204 Center Square Road, Bridgeport, NJ 08014. Winners need not be present. For winners list (available in June, 1996), send a self-addressed, stamped envelope by 1/15/96 to: Dream Come True Winners, P.O. Box 572, Gibbstown, NJ 08027.

THE FOLLOWING APPLIES TO THE SWEEPSTAKES ABOVE:

No purchase necessary. No photocopied or mechanically reproduced entries will be accepted. Not responsible for lost, late, misdirected, damaged, incomplete, illegible, or postage-die mail. Entries become the property of sponsors and will not be returned.

Winner(s) will be notified by mail. Winner(s) may be required to sign and return an affidavit of eligibility/release within 14 days of date on notification or an alternate may be selected. Except where prohibited by law, entry constitutes permission to use of winners' names, hometowns, and likenesses for publicity without additional compensation. Void where prohibited or restricted. All federal, state, provincial, and local laws and regulations apply.

All prize values are in U.S. currency. Presentation of prizes may vary; values at a given prize level will be approximately the same. All taxes are winners' responsibility.

Canadian residents, in order to win, must first correctly answer a time-limited skill testing question administered by mail. Any litigation regarding the conduct and awarding of a prize in this publicity contest by a resident of the province of Quebec may be submitted to the Regie des loteries et courses du Quebec.

Sweepstakes is open to legal residents of the U.S., Canada, and Europe (in those areas where made available) who have received this offer.

Sweepstakes in sponsored by Ventura Associates, 1211 Avenue of the Americas, New York, NY 10036 and presented by independent businesses. Employees of these, their advertising agencies and promotional companies involved in this promotion, and their immediate families, agents, successors, and assignees shall be ineligible to participate in the promotion and shall not be eligible for any prizes covered herein. SWP 3/95

DON'T MISS THESE FABULOUS BANTAM WOMEN'S FICTION TITLES

On Sale in December

BREAKFAST IN BED

by New York Times *bestselling author* Sandra Brown

Sandra Brown captures the wrenching dilemma of a woman tempted by an unexpected—and forbidden—love. Don't miss this classic Bantam publication available in hardcover. ____ 10015-7 $17.95/$24.95 Canada

VANITY *by rising star* Jane Feather

From the incomparable author of the national bestsellers *Violet* and *Valentine* comes a new triumph of romance, brimming with passionate emotion and compelling adventure. ____ 57248-2 $5.99/$7.99

DEATH ELIGIBLE *by the highly acclaimed* Judith Henry Wall

A family is held together by bonds stronger than the law. But what happens when that family must make a choice to give up one of its own? In this mesmerizing new novel, Judith Henry Wall asks this provocative question as she plumbs the depths of one family's secret heart. ____ 56788-8 $5.99/$7.99

SAXON BRIDE *by* Tamara Leigh

Saxon Bride is an electrifying medieval romance in which a woman falls in love with an avenging Norman warrior. But soon a burning passion between them is fanned to life . . . one that could put the Saxon woman's innocent heart in peril. ____ 56534-6 $5.50/$6.99

Now available in paperback

NIGHT SINS ____ 56451-X $5.99/$7.99

by the new master of modern suspense

Tami Hoag

"A knuckle-whitening, spine-chilling thriller." —*New Woman*

Ask for these books at your local bookstore or use this page to order.

Please send me the books I have checked above. I am enclosing $____ (add $2.50 to cover postage and handling). Send check or money order, no cash or C.O.D.'s, please.

Name ______________________________

Address ______________________________

City/State/Zip ______________________________

Send order to: Bantam Books, Dept. FN158, 2451 S. Wolf Rd., Des Plaines, IL 60018

Allow four to six weeks for delivery.

Prices and availability subject to change without notice. FN 158 12/95